.........And Then We Laughed

L Guerin-Cameron

Publisher: ZAAS

Copyright 2010 by Lenore Cameron

All rights reserved.

Published in the United States by

ISBN-10 : 0615671527

EAN-13 : 9780615671529

.........And Then We Laughed

L Guerin-Cameron

Dedication

This book is written in memory of my beloved parents Frederick Julian Guerin and Lucie Angela Guerin Whose dedication and hard work gave our family the security, discipline, love and confidence to navigate the sometimes choppy waters of life. At the same time they gave us the freedom and opportunity to grow as individuals; learning our lessons in the midst of great joy and laughter.

Acknowledgements

I wish to acknowledge my six siblings who not only provided the foundation for my stories, but who with loyalty and incredible humor, have formed bonds that have endured for decades and continue to sustain us as a family.

Most of all, I want to acknowledge the unflinching support and loving encouragement of my husband Eric, my sons Blaine and Julian and my daughter-in-law Marsha. Their enthusiasm and love gave me the confidence to complete this work.

Contents

Friends

I was looking forward to the move from Belmont, but there were people I would miss. At the top of this list were Amelia and Annie. They lived in a little alley near to our house, and I would no longer be able to spend time with them once my family moved away. We were close yet I had never been to their home. I had seen their home in the alley only once, when I went with my brother to take them home. My parents would never have allowed me into that alley without a very good reason... and in all the years that I lived in Belmont, accompanying my brother that day, to take Amelia and Annie home, was the only good reason that ever presented itself.

These two little girls were the prettiest and most adorable children I knew. Annie was rosy cheeked, pleasant, and plump like a baby. She was always smiling; but then she was always happy. She had no reason to be otherwise. Everyone let her have her way including Amelia, who was three years older than Annie, her protector and greatest fan. Amelia was younger than I was, but a little older than my sister Julie, nicknamed Lul, who was five years

1

my junior. Annie was the youngest of us all. Lul shared my friendship with Amelia and Annie for the years that we lived in Belmont, Trinidad, in the late 1950s.

Annie was like our own live doll. Amelia treated her as such and we all catered to her every need. We hugged her all the time and someone was always trying to lift her up. Amelia was not only very protective of Annie, but operated in that big sister role with great maturity. We were led to believe that Annie was her mother's favorite and that if anything were to happen to her, Amelia would reap severe consequences. That might have been true, but it was very evident that Amelia was also crazy about her little sister and was proud to take care of her.

Despite the differences in our ages, the girls seemed always happy to come to our home to play with us. They seemed to know when we would be at home and would just show up at the gate—sometimes within minutes of our arrival. They visited on weekends, after school, (they did not go to our school) after Christmas, or when my sister or I had celebrated a birthday and there were new dolls, tea sets, and new story books. We were always happy to see them and enjoyed every minute we spent together.

Amelia and Annie's mother, Maggie, who looked like she was in her 30s, was a very pretty and very friendly woman of the order of Matt Dillon's Ms. Kitty, but without the saloon. She was slim and had a smooth, olive complexion. Her hair was thick and luscious, and just long enough to be sexy. Something about her laughter was sensuous and she moved and spoke to others as if she was always flirting with them.

Maggie had two older daughters who looked like her sisters rather than her daughters. To my innocent child's mind, they looked like they were in their 20s. Years later, as an adult, I concluded that they probably were.

Patty, one of the girls, was flamboyant and loud with more than a hint of vulgarity in her expressions. Like her mother, she was very pretty. Patty was taller than average, with a slim, very shapely body. She had soft, thick hair that was unnaturally black and was a strong and attractive contrast against her flawless skin. Skimpy tight clothing was Patty's trademark. Once, in the middle of the morning, I saw her shopping for cigarettes in what I was sure was a nightgown, yet she was as much at ease in those clothes as anything else that she wore. It was rumored in the neighborhood that Patty made her living by engaging in the oldest profession. It was a fact that she worked nights; it was a fact that she was not a nurse or a security guard; and it was a fact that there were few other night jobs for women in the capital city of Port of Spain the late 1950s.

Patty was someone whose every movement or statement challenged others. She was distrustful of people and I was afraid of her from the time they moved into the area. I was only 9 years old at that time, but even then, I could sense that she disapproved of the friendship between her little sisters and my family. When the girls visited us, it was usually their mother, Maggie, who would come to get them. She would stand by the wall and call them cheerfully, and she would embrace them as they left through the gate. She would also smile broadly with us, thank us for having the girls over, and they all would wave as they walked away.

Occasionally, instead of Maggie, Patty would come to get the girls. When she did, she spoke to no one in my family. She would come to the gate and call out to Amelia in her too-loud voice that we would hear immediately, even if we were in the back yard. When the girls went to her, waving goodbye to us, she avoided making eye contact with anyone and shepherded them hurriedly in front of her, puffing large deliberate circles of smoke into the air as she strode defiantly toward the alley.

Amelia and Annie's other big sister, I was told, was Patty's twin. They were not identical, and the resemblance between the two was marginal. This sister, whose name I cannot remember, was not as tall as Patty. She too, had black hair, which she wore long— except for bangs that almost covered her eyes. Her demeanor was as different from her twin sister's as her appearance. Patty's twin kept her head down a lot and she never came to pick up her younger siblings from our home. She did not go out very much, and except for cordial pleasantries, I never saw her in conversation with anyone. She did not smile much either and appeared to be shy. Amelia and Annie seemed to love Patty, but they did not speak much of this other sister.

Everyone in this family was light in complexion, had European features and long, straight hair. They were clearly of mixed race— one of the races being Caucasian. Based only on the physical appearance of this family, one could easily assume that they lived in a big house in a nice middle-class neighborhood in Trinidad. They did not.

Class and status in Trinidad, during the 1950s and 1960s, were determined by factors similar to those in other western stratified societies with occupation, education, and family background being the primary criteria. In reality, race had more influence on class-standing in colonial Trinidad than the other three factors combined. People of European ancestry were generally at the top of the social strata, while those of African origin were nearest the bottom. People of mixed race were relegated to various levels within the social pyramid based on their physical attributes. In general, on the sliding scale of white to dark, those who were lighter in complexion with Anglo-Saxon features ranked closer to white and were afforded greater privileges than their darker counterparts. The darkest people, typically those with the most distinctly African features, were in the lowest and the poorest class. The alley in which Amelia and her family lived was populated by very low income, lower class people. Some were honest and hard-working; others engaged in illegal and illicit activities, for which they may or may not have served time.

Despite their physical appearance, Amelia's family seemed at ease with their neighbors in the alley. Everyone, both in and outside the alley, was curious about the family's presence there. Rumors abounded, but nothing was known for sure, about the family's history. Some of the rumors had the mother hiding in the alley from her rich, Venezuelan ex-lover, Pedro, whom everyone knew would never venture near, let alone enter the alley even if he knew where they were. The allegation was that the family had fled because Pedro had become romantically involved with Patty, who had confessed their affair to her mother. Her mother had forgiven her the indiscretion, but resolved to leave Pedro as soon as the opportunity presented itself. One day while Pedro was at work, Maggie took the children and sought refuge in the alley. Another story was that Pedro discovered that Amelia was not his daughter, as he had been led to believe, and had threatened to kill Maggie. In this version of the story, the two adult daughters had not been living with the family, but reunited to support Maggie when her life was threatened. There was also the rumor that Annie's father was a rich married man, who had no children with his wife. He confessed to his wife that, many years before, he had fathered a child through an affair with Maggie. When he took Annie to meet his wife, she fell in love with the child immediately and pressured her husband to file for custody away from Maggie. According to some, it was this threat that drove Maggie and her family into the alley.

Oddly enough, the various rumors about the family's flight to the alley involved three of Maggie's four children. There was no explanation or rumor that mentioned Patty's twin. In retrospect, it appeared that she was not interesting enough even for the rumor mill to take note of, or memorable enough for me to form even a youthful impression of her as an individual in her own right, with a name. Sadly, I remember her only as Patty's twin.

The twins did not have the same father as the little girls and even the two little girls may not have had the same father either. That was as much fact as was ever determined. Amelia's mother may have wanted to keep her younger daughters away from the life of the alley, hence the reason she encouraged their friendship with my family. My father was a professional and our family was solidly middle class. Patty, on the other hand, seemed to resent us and was displeased that her sisters frequented our home and seemed to enjoy being with us. Maggie prevailed and the girls remained close to us from the time they moved into the neighborhood until we moved away.

When we moved, Amelia and Annie spent an entire weekend with us. Lul and I begged our mother for weeks to have the girls come for a visit. We had really missed them in our new home and in our life. When my mother finally made the arrangements, we were very excited and spent hours planning and changing the plans for what we would do when they came. In the end, the plans went better than expected. We were not at all disappointed and neither were they.

On the Friday night that they came, we played with dolls and new board games and we had a difficult time falling asleep. We were all just too excited. Amelia and Annie had played with us for many hours in our old home, but this was the first time they were sleeping over. That first night Annie cried because she missed her mother. At first we could not comfort her, but then my mother took her for a while and did her mom thing and when she came back to bed with us she was just fine.

The next day my aunt took us all to the circus which was in town. What we remember, even more than the circus performances, were the different kinds of sweet foods we were allowed to eat. This aunt was my father's youngest sister. She had no children of her own at that time and was very indulgent. That outing was the highlight of our weekend.

All day Sunday we played and invented games and by the time Amelia and Annie left that night, we had worn ourselves out completely. I remember being very sad when we said goodbye. After they drove off, Lul and I cried. That weekend was the last time any of us ever saw those two beautiful girls.

Less than two weeks after our weekend together, a prominent lawyer who lived less than a half mile from the alley in Belmont where the girls lived, was found by his wife, dead in their bed one morning after she returned from an overnight visit with her ailing mother. Her husband's hands were tied with a bright colored scarf that smelled of cigarette smoke and his body was covered with bright red lipstick. Otherwise he was naked. Neither the scarf nor the lipstick belonged to his wife. By noon the death was being talked about by everyone. It took two days for the coroner to rule that the death was caused by natural causes and for the citizenry to add that he went in ecstasy to his maker. The man had died from a heart attack. The activity that had strained his heart was not an offence to be heard in a court of law, but the court of public opinion can be more intimidating than the law.

Patty did not wait for the coroner's report or the judgment of the court of public opinion. She knew that the scarf could be identified as hers, so the night before the funeral, she and her family packed everything and moved out of the alley to a place as mysterious as the one from which they had come.

Our Fergus

There were people in the old neighborhood with whom I did not have a personal relationship like I did with Amelia and Annie, but who were very memorable in other ways. Some were notable because they were so colorful; others, for other reasons. These people may not have seemed important during the years that I lived among them, but they were embedding themselves in my memory, and I would carry them with me to my new home and beyond. One such person was Fergus.

Fergus was known only by one name. It may have been his first name or his last, I never knew which, and somehow I never considered it to be relevant. As I look through the eyes of an adult, I know now that Fergus was not the old drunk I thought he was at the time. A drunk he was, but old he was not. In all probability, Fergus was less than 35 years old. I don't know that I ever put an exact number to him at the time, but I know I never thought of him as young at all; and he was indeed.

Fergus was of medium height and build with a rugged and very dark complexion. His gait was never steady; his speech was seldom clear; he was also never completely sober. On most days Fergus could be found seated in a corner of a very small shop located next to the most popular candy store in the district. When Fergus was in the store, he was usually quiet and sat facing the door. Mr. Clark, the proprietor of the store, would converse with him from the other side of the counter. I use the term "converse" loosely, because neither one ever really said very much. I don't believe Fergus slurred much then, but he spoke so softly that it was hard to be sure. It was only early in the day that Fergus could be found here in that position. It was only early in the day that Fergus spoke without a slur.

I don't know if Fergus was quiet and subdued in the morning because he had received a good night's rest or not. Truth be told, I never thought of Fergus as having a good night's rest because I never thought of him as having a home and a bed in which to rest. I couldn't conceive of him having a family or even real friends. As far as I knew, Fergus existed only during working hours and only in the immediate environs of Mr. Clark's shop. As the day wore on and he became more intoxicated, he would come onto the sidewalk and offer his social side, which would generally be rejected by passersby, except for the regulars who would provide him with the means to replenish his cup and reduce his sobriety even further. This was Fergus' routine every day that Mr. Clark's shop was open. The shop, like most businesses at that time, closed at 8 p.m. on Saturday nights and remained closed on Sundays.

There was a rumor that sought to explain Fergus' apparent homelessness and general circumstances. According to the story, Fergus was a very smart boy, loved books, and did very well in school. His social skills with his peers, however, were underdeveloped. Fergus endeared himself to adults and was a favorite with his teachers. He spent his free time reading and avoided children his age. His father, a gruff and poorly educated man, was intolerant of Fergus' inability to make friends. He spoke to his wife about it and accused her of encouraging their son's anti-social behavior. His father expressed his concern that Fergus' closeness to his mother and sisters would make him become *funny*, as he put it. He insisted that Fergus be made to engage in *manly activities*. When his wife seemed to ignore his demands, Fergus' father took matters into his own hands.

It was cricket season. Cricket was and still is a very popular sport in Trinidad. It was brought by the British to their colonies and caught on fiercely among the natives. Fergus' father bought him a brand new cricket bat, and although Fergus had not expressed any interest in the sport, his father knew that the brand new bat would bring his son instant friends. He knew also that the game might be his son's entrance into the social world of young boys and away from books and the women in the family, thereby ensuring that Fergus would not grow up to be *funny*.

Fergus' father escorted him to the field where he knew boys would be gathered on Saturday afternoon with their crooked homemade bats. He practically pushed the reluctant Fergus, bat in hand, onto the field and let him know that he would be watching. As expected, it was not long before Fergus and his new bat became the center of attention, and most welcomed into the game. Actually, his bat was welcomed; Fergus was just a necessary accompaniment.

On the sidelines, Fergus' father smiled smugly and was pleased that his plan was working. His son was engaging in a manly sport with children of his own age. Fergus had been extremely clumsy at the wicket, but his father expected this would change in time. He envisaged his son swinging and running—a star in the making—playing in the ever-so-popular Test Cricket matches, bating inning after inning, and the two of them bonding and sharing the joy of the sport. What actually happened, according to the story, was quite different. Within ten minutes of his new activity, a ball flew through the air in Fergus' direction, and as clumsy and slow as he was, Fergus was unable to get out of the way in time. The ball connected very forcefully with his right temple, he fell to the ground instantly and was unconscious for several minutes.

His father, initially more irritated than concerned, put him in his car and took him home. Fergus seemed to be okay for the next two days, and then his seizures began. These seizures continued, getting more violent and lasting longer. After having a seizure, Fergus would be disoriented and confused. Sometimes he was unable to respond intelligently for long periods. It is not clear what the exact diagnosis of his condition was, or what, if any treatment was given to him. What is known, is that he missed a lot of school because of the seizures and began to fall behind in his classes. His ability to learn seemed to become severely diminished and with no special education available to him, he ceased to perform well in school. Eventually he stopped going to school altogether. At home he spoke very little, stopped reading as much as he used to, and then when reading became very difficult, he stopped reading altogether. He regressed somewhat in his general performance and had no interest in anything at all.

His mother blamed his father for what happened. His father blamed his mother, but only weakly. More than likely he too blamed himself. He took to drinking, stopped speaking to Fergus, and barely even looked at him. The family began to collapse and then the father made a clean break, leaving the family behind. The mother assumed the role of head of household, but did so with great bitterness. She too began to distance herself emotionally from Fergus. She was forced to take a job to support the family, which left her very little time to spend with him. His older sister stayed loyal to him. She loved and supported him through it all. When she got married and left home, Fergus was completely isolated. Then, when he was old enough to leave the house without permission, he found a new home in Mr. Clark's shop and a new best friend in rum—a friend that stayed loyal to him all of his life.

On some Saturday nights after Mr. Clark's shop was closed, or after the largess of others had been exhausted, Fergus would call at our gate. I don't know if Fergus had any income of his own, or any independent means of supporting his alcoholism, but I do know that when all else failed, we were a part of his back-up plan. He would stand at our gate and call, and continue to call, even when we tried to ignore him. Fergus knew that once we let him in, he was assured of being able to *tie one on* with my father, who had himself, just returned from many happy hours. A significant difference between the two was that my dad's drinking was confined to weekends and with his friends.

My father had taught Fergus in elementary school, and this history was the source of all of his communication with my father on those Saturday nights. Once through the gate, Fergus did not even pretend to go through the social chit chat like, "How are you?" or "How are things going?" or even "How are the wife and children?" that is customary with a visit. There was not one minute wasted before Fergus got to the drinking. My father knew that he and Fergus had no grounds for friendship. He knew why Fergus had come, so he too went directly to offering the drink, taking only one himself to be polite. Drinking for him was a social activity shared with friends and Fergus was not his friend.

Fergus reminisced about school, as he swallowed shot after shot of free hot rum. Fergus never took ice in his drinks, perhaps because he could drink faster without ice or maybe, because this way he eliminated the opportunity for someone not having ice, to use that as an excuse for not giving him a drink. Refrigerators were small and slow in those days and ice was not always readily available.

Fergus had the same routine every time he visited. He would remind my dad of the *licks* he used to give his students (corporal punishment was a routine part of school discipline then). He would recall the *licks* he got personally, and he would recall that my father taught him two poems in particular: *The Daffodils* by William Wordsworth and *The Day is Done* by Henry Wadsworth Longfellow. To show that the lessons had been well learned, Fergus would recite—through thickly slurred speech—these poems or parts thereof, over and over, generously punctuating his recitation with, "Mr. Guerin, yuh remember? Eh, Mr. Guerin? You remember how you did beat we for that?" Then he would continue, or begin again:

"The day is done, and darkness
Falls from the wings of Night.
As a feather is wafted downwards
From an eagle in his flight...

Mr. Guerin, yuh remember those days? Eh? Yuh remember?" At this point there would be another shot of rum taken, some indistinguishable babble, and then he would either repeat the verse or lapse into his next poem:

"I wandered lonely as a cloud
That floats on high o'er vales and hills,
When all at once I saw a crowd,
A host of golden daffodils..."

I don't recall that he ever got further than those lines in those particular poems before he reverted to, "Mr. Guerin, yuh remember? Eh, Mr. Guerin? Yuh eh play, yuh did beat we for that yuh know. Yuh remember, Mr. Guerin?" It seemed necessary to repeat my dad's name as often as he could, for reasons only the happy drunk could understand.

During his career my father had taught countless boys who went on to become successful adults. Many of them visited with him over the years. Always, they were respectful and despite the years, continued to maintain great decorum and a certain social distance with their old teacher. Many came by proudly presenting their achievements and even brought their families. Often they would make reference to their days as dad's students and often they would tell us children what dad was like as a teacher, the discipline he instilled, and the standards he set. Dad always seemed pleased to have his old students visit and share their new lives. He was happy to hear of their experiences and success and he expressed this with enthusiasm. During the episodes with Fergus, on the other hand, I don't recall that my father ever said anything other than, "Yes Fergus, yes Fergus, I remember." He would smile and watch Fergus and I know he noted his grammar. I suspect he regretted that Fergus had not grasped the English language with the same efficacy that he had grasped English literature.

The Brown Uniforms

There was a family in my old neighborhood that my brother and I were very happy to leave. This was a small family that lived several houses away from us. We knew only the mother and two daughters, although we never knew their names, and we referred to both girls only as the *Brown Uniforms*. The girls attended a Methodist school and wore brown pleated overalls over cream blouses. Both girls were unkempt and the combination of their dark, somber uniform, scruffy socks, and dirty shoes elicited negative responses from nearly everyone. The *Brown Uniforms* had a habit of boldly staring at people—an anti-social characteristic that many people in that era often associated with limited mental capacity. Whenever the girls spoke...well...they really didn't speak, they shouted in a loud, uncouth way that was offensive to everyone within earshot. Their reputation was irrevocably ruined by their proclivity for swearing and their involvement in fist fights, not only with other girls in their school and neighborhood but also with older boys. Once, when my younger brother, Allan, was on the street alone, he encountered these two. No one in my family had ever actually had any altercation with them, but our mere existence would have been enough to make us deadly enemies of theirs.

My father had a steady job as a school principal, we always had a car, and we all went to prestigious Catholic schools. We had a solid, well-built, painted, concrete house. My mother did not work outside the home and we were always clean, happy, and well-liked in the neighborhood. Any one of these factors would have been sufficient to make us disliked by the *Brown Uniforms*; with these factors combined, my siblings and I were marked targets for their aggression.

A person's complexion played a role in their social status and how they were received by others. Unfortunately, this is still prevalent in many African American communities in the U.S. and in other countries throughout the diaspora, where native peoples were colonized and enslaved. Since the Europeans were, by force and design, economically and socially superior to the people they colonized, they were almost always the standard; others were measured by their closeness to, or distance from this standard. Consequently, people of obvious "mixed" European ancestry were held in higher esteem than people with "purer" native roots and almost every citizen of African origin could trace some part of their ancestry back to Europe. Some roots led to the white slave masters, but however the mixture came about, Europeans changed not only the landscape, but the DNA of the inhabitants of the countries they colonized. Trinidad was an example of such change. In theory, therefore, most citizens were of mixed race. In reality however, those considered "mixed" by the citizens of the country, were those who were very light in complexion and whose hair was no longer the wooly texture of Africans, but was smooth or curly.

My family was not "mixed" so that was not a factor in our relationship with the *Brown Uniforms*; but that aside, there was no denying the socio-economic differences. The *Brown Uniforms* knew it. We did too. No matter what our individual responses to them might have been, we were perceived as mortal enemies; our fate with the *Brown Uniforms* was sealed.

My brother, Allan, was generally not a trouble maker, so everyone believed that he did not say or do anything to the *Brown Uniforms* on the day of the altercation. He had been walking in the vicinity of their home when they were both standing in the gap. As he approached them, for no known reason, they made as if to hit him. Then, as he speedily distanced himself from their reach, they began to hurl stones in his general direction. The stones hit the walls, the street, and sidewalk around him, but none hit him. I suspect they deliberately aimed to scare him, but not hurt him. Despite their guile, they may have had the good sense to know that hurting one of us would not have gone over lightly with my parents or the community in general. Whatever their intentions were, they managed to instill a deadly fear, not only in Allan, but in me as well. Whenever I had to pass near the driveway to their home, I would run as fast as I could. Crossing to the other side of the street would have given more distance from the *Brown Uniforms*, but that presented another danger.

In the years about which I write, homelessness was unknown on the island in which I lived. There were, of course, characters who were clearly insane and preferred to walk the streets in their respective areas, talking to themselves; driving imaginary cars; pushing, never riding, heavily decorated bikes; or dancing in the street scantily clad. But all of these persons had roofs under which to shelter at nightfall. Except for the woman who slept on the sidewalk directly across from the driveway where the *Brown Uniforms* lived, people did not live and sleep on the sidewalk.

This vagrant (a word never used to describe her at that time) slept on cardboard boxes laid against the wall of the building that housed a hardware store. She wore rags and frequently during her waking hours, rummaged through a few cardboard boxes that stayed at the foot of her makeshift bed. These boxes were filled with junk that she seemed to reorganize on a regular basis. She was a contemptible and hostile woman who glared murderously at anyone who walked even near the sidewalk where she housed her possessions. She was obscene and abusive to anyone whose voice or movement disturbed her daytime nap. I was as afraid of her as I was of the *Brown Uniforms*, and getting to and from school, the pharmacy or the greengrocers, and most other business places always meant, for me, running the gauntlet.

We had lived in fear of the *Brown Uniforms* and the vagrant for many years before we found out that the vagrant's choice of that particular piece of real estate was not random. The fact that she had the phenotype and genotype of the *Brown Uniforms* was not just because she shared the same race and geography. The vagrant was the maternal aunt of the *Brown Uniforms*. The original story, told by one reliable and very old resident of the area, gives very few details. The general gist of the story is that the vagrant, whose name was never given, once lived with the *Brown Uniforms*. She had no husband or children of her own. It was very uncommon in those days for a single woman to live alone, or with other single women. They always remained with parents or moved in with siblings as part of their extended family. One day, the story continues, the vagrant had a very serious quarrel with her sister's family. It was not known by that reporter what the quarrel was about, but as a result of it, she was thrown out of the family home. Thereupon, she took up residence on the sidewalk where she would be in full view of her family and they would be in her view as well. If she intended that seeing her on the sidewalk across the street, every time they walked down the driveway from their home, would bring about some remorse on their part—reconciliation and reinstatement for her—she was wrong. She remained on her cardboard mat on the sidewalk for as many years as I could recall, and the only interaction with her nieces was obscene and abusive, with all parties expressing only mutual contempt.

As often happens, what is not known is invented; so it was with the story of the family of the *Brown Uniforms*. A reporter, less reliable than the original source, said that the quarrel with the aunt involved ownership of the property on which the family lived. It is said that the property was the original home of the two adult sisters. They had lived with their parents and one brother, who died under mysterious circumstances. After his death, the younger sister left home and was gone for a couple of years. She was known to be in domestic service to a white family in the south of the island. During her absence, her older sister got married and her husband moved into the family home. Shortly thereafter, the first of the *Brown Uniforms* was born.

This new branch of the family, older daughter, husband, and baby began to assume more and more control of the home. The elderly parents had never stopped grieving for their son and did not object to their daughter and her husband running the home. It was as if the young couple owned the house and the older couple lived with them. Their role in the home and even in their own lives was controlled by the young family. The older couple was isolated and confined to a small room in the house. Their meals were brought to them at the convenience of their older daughter. The young couple was very comfortable and their family began to grow. The second of the *Brown Uniforms* was born just one year after the first and the family seemed to be doing well. The father of the *Uniforms* had a reasonably good job at the railway; the mother made candy, which she sold to a small shop nearby. Meanwhile, the isolated older couple grew feeble and disconnected from society, as their daughter did not allow them visitors. They also had very little interaction with their grandchildren, and they rarely received letters from their younger daughter living in the south of the island.

One day, the young husband was boarding a moving train at the main station in the city, to do a required job inspection. He lost his footing and fell. On the way down, he hit his head on an iron post and died on the spot. His death was big news on the island. Pictures of the deceased, his wife, and children were featured on the front pages of the leading newspapers. His sudden notoriety was not due to job rank or importance in the community, but based solely on the fact that he was a young employee of the railroad.

His widow's sister read the news of his death, while in the kitchen of the house in which she had been working. She gave notice to her employers immediately, packed her meager belongings, and returned to her family home. Whatever may have caused her to leave, almost three years before, did not get in the way of the enthusiasm with which her parents greeted her on her return. They were elated to have her back, and she, in turn, made up for her absence by showering them with care. She helped to integrate them back into the community and looked after them until their deaths. They died within six weeks of each other and less than two years from the death of their son-in-law.

Now the two sisters and the two young children remained in the house together, and from all accounts, the relationships were civil. There was no great warmth or affection in the home, but the sisters were cordial to each other with little verbal communication taking place. After their parents' deaths, the younger sister got a job in a nearby grocery store while the rest of the family got by on the monthly check that came from the government via a fund known as the "widows and orphans fund." It was a benefit to which they were entitled as a result of the job that the deceased husband had with the railroad.

One day the older sister presented to her younger sister, a document that gave her full ownership of the family home. She said that she was showing it to her sister to correct any expectations of joint ownership. She said that their paretheir had given the property to her while they were still alive, because she had been taking care of them and was expected to do so until their deaths. The younger sister, not believing that their parents had done so, declared the document a forgery and continued to live in the home as before—for more than a year.

On the second anniversary of their mother's death, the younger sister accused the older sister of killing their parents. The accusation seemed to come out of nowhere and gave rise to very hostile responses from the accused. The quarrel escalated in volume and intensity. When, in addition to this, the younger sister accused the older one of stealing the house and her birthright, the neighbors say the quarrel became violent and went on throughout the evening, into the night, and continued until dawn. At daybreak, the younger sister was physically removed from the property and took up residence on the sidewalk where she remained in full view of the family. When my family moved into the area, she was already in residence on the sidewalk. Three years later, when we left, she was still there.

Moving Day

*I*t was my first time taking public transportation, my first time seeing Hosay, and my first day walking to our new home in St James. It was July 4, 1960. I was 11 years old, anxious and excited about all the firsts. I did not know what to expect from the bus ride or the experience of Hosay, before the actual day, but I had been eagerly anticipating the move to the new house for several weeks. I had not seen the new house before we moved and I was unfamiliar with the area, even though it was less than five miles from the old house.

There had been several other moves in my short lifetime. Three years earlier we had moved to the house in Belmont—the one we were now leaving. That move was also in July, and just days before my First Communion. I was eight years old then, and I don't recall that I experienced the same excitement as I did with this move to St James. Besides, I had been familiar with Belmont before we actually moved there to live, because I was already going to school in the area. That move was not to unknown territory, as it was now. I was fully acquainted with the house in Belmont long before we moved in, as the house had been my mother's family home and my parents had owned it for many years. My two older siblings and I were born there, and though I left the house before I was old enough to remember it, I was aware of it; I had passed the house many times in my daily activities and knew that one day my family and I would return to it. We had left that house in Belmont the first time only to live closer to my father's job. He was assigned to work in the rural districts for several years and commuting from the house in Belmont was inconvenient and impractical. This move to St. James was very different. We had every expectation that it would be permanent. Our family had grown since we first lived in Belmont and we needed more space. We had, in every way, outgrown our Belmont roots.

In preparation for leaving Belmont, I remember helping my mother to wrap glasses and dishes in newspaper so that they could be packed securely. For days, I went through the drawers with my clothes taking out any torn garments that could not be repaired, garments with worn elastic, and those that did not fit well anymore. Those in the third category were set aside to hand down to my younger sister; those in categories one and two were discarded.

The day we actually moved was a very rainy one. Our furniture and household items had been moved while my siblings and I were at school, and we were to go to the new house after dismissal. I usually walked home with my older sister, Lyn, and her friends. That day there was only one friend—Ann. Except for Ann, who lived close to the new house in St. James—some miles away from our school—all our school friends lived in Belmont near to the house we were leaving. This distance from school now would require us to take public transportation to get home. I say Ann was a "friend" because she had been my sister's friend for years, but at the time of the move to St James, she and my sister were not on speaking terms. Nevertheless, the three of us took the Roxy bus, as it was called, to the last stop. From there, Lyn and I had just over a quarter of a mile walk to our new home.

It was pouring heavily when we got off the bus. Ann opened her umbrella and invited me to join her under it. My sister, however, walked a few steps ahead of us, pretending that she did not care about being drenched by the downpour, but it must have been awkward and even embarrassing for her. Without her usual group of friends that first day, she seemed alone and dejected. Usually, she was the center of attention, telling stories and holding everyone interest- bound. I knew she resented having to be responsible for me, having me underfoot, and within earshot of all that went on with her and her friends. Most of Lyn's friends were a year or so older than she was and almost four years older than I was. Sometimes, to further assert herself in her group, she would make fun of me, and her friends would be amused. Today, I felt avenged for all those times when she was a star at my expense, and those times were many.

What helped to make that rainy day so memorable was that it was one of the days of the Hosay celebration in St. James. The road was blocked to all vehicular traffic and I was mesmerized by the huge crowds milling around us, the towering bamboo temples that seemed to touch the sky, and the red and green moons that dipped and swayed with the dancers to the beat of the drums. Unknown to me, the spectacle unfolding before us was the last day of Hosay—a religious festival celebrated on the anniversary date that Hussein and Hassan, the martyred grandsons of the prophet Mohammed, were killed defending Islam 1,400 years before in Persia, (now known as Iraq).

Hosay started as a Muslim mourning festival—first celebrated in Trinidad in 1854. It followed the East Indian indentured laborers, who had migrated to the tiny island just a decade before, from Lucknow (a Shiite city in India). The festival had symbolic and religious value to these Muslims and was the center of their cultural existence. By 1960, it acquired broader, secular appeal for Trinidadians of all ethnic groups, who welcomed yet another opportunity to celebrate and dance in the street.

The Hosay celebration lasts three days and nights. The first night on the street is Flag Night. As the name suggests, flags are paraded through the streets by each of the Mumbas. The second night is called Little Hosay. On this night, small Tadjahs are paraded in the streets. The finale is Kabala Day or Big Hosay. The full-size Tadjahs are brought into the streets and paraded for public view for the first time, accompanied by the half-moons and Tassa drums. After the Hosay parade is over and the symbols are cast out to sea. After the spectacle of that day, I looked forward to witnessing the entire event the following year, and in the years to come.

In all my years growing up in Trinidad & Tobago, I had not been as exposed to East Indian culture as I was that afternoon and as I would be for the next decade of my life. It was a decade in which I grew into a teenager and then a young adult; a decade in which I experienced great happiness; a decade to which I always go, when I recall my youth and my life in Trinidad.

To me, growing up in Trinidad was growing up in St James. What went before is too distant, and what came after was not as significant. It is the decade in which the values learned and the memories created shaped my entire life. It is a decade in which I remember little but laughter and a loving family; joy, fun, and great friends; safety and security. It is the decade in which I discovered and embraced not only Hosay, but learned to appreciate and became a part of the special culture of St James.

***

The move to St James I said was all positive because that is what I thought since I didn't have to leave my old school and I could still see my friends. There was no fear of making new friends or sadness at leaving old ones, except of course Amelia and Annie. As a child, I could not and did not know that my mother had to "pull strings" at the bank so that my father could finance the new home. She accomplished this through a network of contacts that extended back to old acquaintances and friends of Pa, her deceased father. Getting a mortgage in the 1960s was no easy feat for an "ordinary" family on a fixed income with seven children and no collateral. At that time, Trinidad was still a colony of Great Britain and the rules and values of the colonial masters still governed the natives.

The house in St. James was twice the value of the Belmont house and the mortgage would have been relatively large for that period. Today, one could not get a good, small, used car for the price that my parents paid for that house. My father was the sole income earner and my mother had few marketable skills. Women were not paid very well in those days, even for the skills they did have. My mother would not have been able to find a job that would have allowed her to pay that mortgage and maintain the family, if my dad was no longer with us or able to work; mortgages were not insured in those days. The situation with the bank and the mortgage, I later learned, went on for quite a while. My mother made many personal appearances to her contacts at the bank, before the loan was secured. I also did not know that my father, unaccustomed to any debt—and worse, a debt of that size—was unable to sleep for many weeks after the purchase, and long after we were happily enjoying our new home and our new neighborhood.

My father's contacts and friends were not in the financial world. His influence lay elsewhere. As a school principal he could help with a transfer to a new school or enrollment of a deserving student in a prestigious school. He also had some friends in high positions in the police department so that, in theory, he could fix a ticket, if his high ethical standards would ever have allowed him to do so. But in the bank, he was out of his element and very clearly and ungraciously subject to my mother's "people."

My mother's father, my grandfather, Pa—who none of us children ever knew—was a civil servant employed with the government on a fixed income. He was a Master Seaman, a qualification he had earned in the U.S. on May 22, 1908, according to the certificate, which we still cherish. Back in his homeland, he married my grandmother and during my mother's childhood and early adolescence, he was the captain of the vessel that transported goods and passengers between the twin islands of Trinidad and Tobago. He later became the Harbor Master stationed at the ports. On his first appointment to the post of Harbor Master, he was stationed in Tobago, which had then and still has today, a rather small port with little commerce except for cruise ships and passenger, and cargo boats from Trinidad. Later he was promoted to the Port in Trinidad. In this position, Grandfather Pa, known to all as Captain John Cadwell Pierre, would not have been considered a man of means. However, he had an industrious father, John Decastro Pierre, also a former public servant. He had invested well and, on his death, left a sizeable inheritance to his son, John Cadwell Pierre, whose whereabouts at the time were reported only as being "in parts beyond the sea." No one was able to locate him to inform him of his father's death, or of the funeral. For all anyone knew he might have been in India, the Ivory Coast, or some other country. As a young man, Grandfather Pa not only traveled extensively, but often stayed and lived in the places where his travels took him.

As the story goes, once Grandfather Pa lived in India for almost two years, because when the ship on which he was a sailor docked in India, he went ashore to explore a nearby city, enjoyed himself so much that he got completely inebriated and when his ship was ready to set sail again, he was nowhere to be found. When he awoke from his drunken state, in a stranger's bed, he had no way of reconnecting with his ship. He had money, so he found a house, and soon was enjoying India with a full staff of domestic servants and new friends. Almost two years later he became involved in a fight with some sailors from a visiting ship. When the police were called and the sailors ran to their ship, my grandfather ran with them, and took off again in an unknown ship, to an unknown destination. He left behind his staff waiting to attend to his needs, as they had done for the two years prior. Grandfather Pa left India as unceremoniously as he had arrived.

On his return to Trinidad—after his father's death—and on receipt of the part of the inheritance of which his god-father, his father's best friend, was not able to defraud him, he became quite comfortable. Because of this inheritance and his talent as an inveterate gambler, he often made large deposits to the bank. Thus, he established very good business as well as social relationships with people of significance at the older banks. When my mother became of age, she secured a position as a bookkeeper at one of the oldest banks and had worked there until she married my father in 1943. By 1960, my grandfather had been deceased for 15 years and even longer been separated from most of his inheritance. My mother's legacy of work was dormant the same number of years. However, she was still able to call on those relationships that had been forged at the bank, to secure the loan needed to purchase the new home.

I did not know that our old house did not sell for the asking price. One reason, I learned later, was that there was no telephone line to the house and the telephone company was unable to connect anything other than a party line to our location. Other structural issues had also reduced its desirability, but it was the telephone problem that was particularly troubling to potential buyers. By 1960, people were getting accustomed to the idea of having telephone services in their homes. Most homes still did not have a telephone but people wanted to have early access to private lines, rather than the party lines that were more readily available. A party line provided telephone service in the home, but it meant sharing that telephone line with another family in the area. Perhaps, in a big impersonal city in the U.S. or Europe, this would not be so daunting a problem, but in Belmont—where the few thousand people already knew too much of each other's business—giving someone access to your phone conversations did not go over very well. One would not know with whom one would share the line, and there were some people with whom sharing a line would be more problematic than others. A telephone arrangement of this kind could be considered a threat rather than a convenience particularly if, for example, one had to share a party line with someone like Ma Lopice.

Ma Lopice

Ma Lopice was a neighbor who spent most of her time sitting on the porch speaking in very loud tones to anyone who would listen. I cannot fathom how a woman with a husband and at least three grandchildren, ages three to seven years, could have so many free hours to sit in a rocker. Perhaps her size—she weighed over 300 pounds—allowed her to be exempt from household duties; maybe she was ill, whatever the explanation, she had a tremendous amount of leisure time which cannot be said to have been used productively. I would not call her a gossip, but I will say that she was always in possession of an inordinate amount of information on the personal lives of people in the area and she was very generous in sharing it with others.

As a young child, my most significant frame of reference for an adult female was my own mother. She charged around the house at great speeds from the time she woke at sun up until she went to bed well into the night. She was constantly on her feet—preparing a meal, cleaning the house, washing or folding clothes—except for the times when she was darning clothes, having a meal, or dressing the smaller children. I was therefore exceedingly puzzled by the fact that Ma Lopice seemed to spend all day in her rocker. I knew that old ladies were allowed that privilege, but Ma Lopice was not an old lady.

Ma Lopice talked to a great deal to the passersby day and got out of her rocker only when Papa, as she called her husband, did not respond to her call, and the gate needed to be unlocked to allow a potential informant to join her on the porch. At those times, her steps were slow and labored and she would be irritated with Papa for not being available to save her the trouble of opening the gate. Ma Lopice was as loud as she was fat. One would always have the impression when she spoke, that the person to whom she was speaking was a great distance away. However, one seldom heard the person shout back. In fact, the other party was generally right on the porch with her or on the sidewalk, which was only a few feet from the porch. One also had the impression that some of these guests may not have intended to visit with Ma Lopice. However, because the sidewalk was so close to her porch, when they were accosted and cornered with the loud talk and pleasant laughter en route to shopping or other errands, retreat was difficult; so they reluctantly entered through the gate.

Ma Lopice was very affectionate with her grandchildren, who Papa dutifully brought to her for her indulgence, every day before and after school. The affectionate term "Papa," which she used for her husband, belied the fact that most of her interaction with him consisted of her giving him orders and complaining when they were not executed to her satisfaction.

Sharing a telephone line with Ma Lopice would have been a fearful proposition, but she was not one of a kind. In small communities, like the one in which we lived, people like her were bred and cultivated and their production was prolific. Ma Lopice was one of many examples of why a party line with anyone was such an unattractive consideration.

Party line notwithstanding, I was surprised that the telephone situation had been such an issue in the sale of the Belmont house. We never had a telephone while we lived there. Of course most of our friends did not have telephones either, so it did not affect us. In those days, children did not depend on technology for entertainment. They used their imaginations; they made up games to play; they made toys from raw material. They attended neighborhood schools, walked home with friends, and played outdoors until dark. They did not know or miss television, air conditioning, or electronic games. A community was not virtual; it was not in cyberspace. We had the designation of a third-world nation, but, we thought that we were on top of the world. We never saw ourselves as primitive; we believed we were original.

The same phenomena that insulated our island consciousness from the pejorative opinions of outsiders, protected us from the harsh realities of adult life. In my eager anticipation of the move, I did not know that the sale of the Belmont house and consequent move to St. James was a major source of anxiety for my parents. I did not know that they had been quarreling over it for weeks. My father was concerned that his salary would not be able to cover the mortgage and continue to pay other living expenses. My mother considered that being "God's child" made mathematical calculations unnecessary and any shortfall would be covered by His grace. These adult concerns had no impact on my 11-year-old life. Children in my household had responsibilities, and yes, they had fears and concerns, but they were fears and concerns about their own childhood issues. We were afraid that our teachers would ask a question in class that we could not answer. We were afraid that we would face further embarrassment, if they shouted at us, or worse, administered corporal punishment. Yes, we went to Catholic school and the nuns, as well as the lay teachers, were allowed to beat us for any infractions that they considered warranted a beating. They were allowed to remove and keep our belt, if it was not the belt prescribed for the uniform. They were allowed to wait at the gate for latecomers and beat them as they entered the school compound. They were allowed to shout our transgressions so loudly that all the other classes and teachers on the floor would hear and feel free to laugh at us.

Children were afraid that a neighbor or anyone who knew them might find their behavior on the street to be unacceptable and relay this to their parent, who would then issue appropriate punishment. In addition, children were afraid to place too low in the end of term exams and that everyone would know this. These were the fears that children had. They did not fear their parents breaking up, or the lights being disconnected for lack of payment. They certainly did not know about bank or mortgage notes or any other issues that their parents were having. Children did not know about these adult problems. In this regard, there was a chasm between the world of the adults and that of children that held the memories and innocent impressions that informed my childhood and so many others during this period.

Miss Pee

My mother had a penchant for keeping old women, who were once friends or acquaintances of her parents, close to our family. Perhaps it was her way of showing us true Christian love. To us, the children, it was certainly a very effective way of making us miserable. These women were mainly non-relatives with whom my mother had been close when her parents were alive, or who had received some form of support from her deceased parents. The only blood relative in this group was the nicest, most fun, least demanding, and the one who very rarely visited. Her name was Auntie Grace. The others were all "characters" in their own right. The most notable, and least liked of these women, was Willemina Pee, known to all her friends as Missy. To my siblings and me, in polite company, she was Auntie Missy; among us, privately, she was Miss Pee.

Every Sunday, my dad would attend 9:30 a.m. mass at the Cathedral of the Immaculate Conception, in the capital city of Port of Spain. We had a parish church much nearer to our home, but the local parish priest tried my father's patience with his controlling personality. This paragon of virtue would stop the service and draw attention to people in the church if they came late, or in some way, did anything that did not meet with his approval. My father was not the kind of person to accept that sort of disrespect, and so rather than allow himself to be tested, he chose to go to mass at the Cathedral, which was much more impersonal, and where he felt comfortable. After mass every week, my dad would dutifully pick up Auntie Missy, who lived nearby in what was then called Marine Square (now Brian Lara Promenade), and bring her to spend the day with us. Her arrival was never welcomed by the children in our home, and I believe my father tolerated her only for my mother's sake and because it meant that he had someone to share a drink or two with after Sunday lunch—Auntie Missy could "hold her liquor like one of the boys."

Auntie Missy was a link to my mother's past as she was an old friend of her parents' and my mother had very little real family left. My mother had a very big heart and an even bigger sense of duty. I believe she also felt sorry for this old woman who had no family life of her own. This is not to say that Auntie Missy did not have a family. In fact, she had an unmarried son and a daughter-in-law—the wife of her older son, who had been killed in war many years earlier—yet she did not have any of the bonding experiences that one would expect from a family unit. She was such a mean and cantankerous old witch, that people did not enjoy being around her. Despite my parents' generosity in opening our home to her, she never seemed to like me or any of my siblings. We are firmly convinced that Miss Pee had spent countless hours devising plots and plans to get us into trouble with our parents.

Once she provoked my brother, Mark, to the point where he physically attacked her and wrestled with her in a confined space in front of the refrigerator. Mark was three years my junior and six years old at the time.

In those days, in my culture, children had an inordinate amount of respect for adults, especially those associated with the family. We responded to them with lowered eyes. We did not initiate conversation with them but waited to be spoken to, and they were always addressed as sir, madam, Mr. or Mrs. Family friends, and sometimes even neighbors, were auntie or uncle. Children did not even defend themselves against an adult, and language was careful and formal. Disrespect to an adult was not tolerated. Therefore, when a seven-year-old not only raised a hand to strike, but engaged in a physical struggle with an adult, it had to have been under dire circumstances. Today, no one recalls what gave rise to the struggle between my brother and Miss Pee, but the incident itself is indelibly etched in the minds of the entire family.

Despite Miss Pee's advanced age, she was a sturdy woman and so it would not be fair to say that the seven-year-old won the fight, but the shock effect of the attack on Miss Pee was sufficient to consider it a win for him.

On another occasion, Elbert, the oldest sibling, was the target of her provocation. This incident we remember well. The family always spent Christmas day with my paternal grandmother and my two spinster aunts in the country district of Sangre Grande, my father's hometown. Another married aunt and my only uncle and their respective spouses and children, our cousins, always joined us for the day.

On Boxing Day, the day after Christmas, which is also a public holiday in Trinidad, the same group would come to our home in Port of Spain for the day to celebrate my parents' wedding anniversary. Usually, on Christmas night when my family went home, one or more of my siblings would remain in Sangre Grande to drive back with an aunt or uncle the next day. An equal number of cousins would travel with my parents on Christmas night. My cousins were close in age to my siblings and me, and we enjoyed spending time together during the holidays. Christmas night was convenient for the parents to arrange for us to be together because we did not live close to each other.

Elbert volunteered to stay over that particular Christmas, but as my parents were about to leave, he had a change of heart and decided that he wanted to go home. By this time, a cousin had taken his place in the car, and not wanting to inconvenience her, he asked my older sister, Lyn, to stay over in his place and allow him to go home. At first Lyn refused, although she had no special reason for staying or for going. Maybe she was just too settled in the car. Elbert persisted but Lyn kept refusing. By this time, everyone who was leaving was seated in the car except, the driver. Elbert pleaded his case with my sister through the open window of the car and Lyn seemed to be weakening in her position as my brother continued to press his point. Without warning, the car window rolled up and a stunned Elbert looked on from the sidewalk, thwarted and confused by this turn of events. Elbert stood motionless, as the window was rolled down ever so slightly revealing the upper portion of Miss Pee's wrinkled face. "I told her not to answer you anymore," she sneered. Just at that moment my father got into the driver's seat, waved goodbye to the relatives, oblivious to the brewing hostility. Elbert (forlorn but angry) rushed toward the slightly opened window and spoke directly to the wrinkled face, in a tone just loud enough for the recipient to hear. "Auntie Missy" he said, "yuh too damn interfering." The car drove off and Elbert bounded up the steps to the verandah to join the other family members as they waved goodbye.

The car had not gone but a few hundred yards when it stopped and reversed. Elbert, still on the verandah, knew he was in trouble, so he rapidly told his story to everyone gathered there. There was no time for reaction. The car was back at the gate; my father was out of the car and purposefully ascended the steps, his hand fingering the buckle of his belt. My Aunt Simona, who we think had always harbored an intense dislike for Miss Pee, put herself between Elbert and my father and interceded with, "Feddie"—that was what my father's mother and siblings called him—"this is Christmas day. You can't beat the boy on Christmas day. Feddie, did you hear the whole story?" The other adults did not speak, but my father sensed that he did not have their support either. He sighed, assured my brother that the matter was not closed and informed him that he would be dealt with the following day.

Ironically, it was Miss Pee herself who unwittingly caused my brother to elude punishment for the disrespect he had shown to her. No sooner had my brother arrived home along with my aunts, cousins, and the rest of the family group that was left behind on Christmas night, than she began to remind my father about executing the punishment. It was the Christmas season, it was my parents' wedding anniversary and we had a houseful of family and guests. So, passing sentence on a juvenile offender, who obviously had been provoked into disrespect, was not foremost on the agenda. At one point in the day, my father was in the middle of toasting or "firing one" with his male buddies, who had dropped by for a drink, when Miss Pee interrupted him to say, "Don't forget about Elbert." Later, when she met my father in the kitchen replenishing the ice bucket to return to his guests, she issued a third reminder. At this point, my father told her in very clear language and undisguised disgust that she was not to remind him of the incident again; not that day; not ever. She never did, and neither did anyone else. No adult ever mentioned the subject to my brother after that, and he was never assigned any form of punishment. Well, Miss Pee may have lost two battles, but she would not concede the war. The next time she came after two of us simultaneously. I was one of the two.

It was the feast of Corpus Christi, a Thursday in the month of May, 1959. According to Catholic tradition in Trinidad, on that day, Catholics turned out in very large numbers to participate in a ceremony, which involved most notably a procession around the Cathedral of the Immaculate Conception. My younger brother, Allan, and I had been sent to dutifully follow the procession. Dehydrated after what seemed like many hours in the blazing sun, we decided to visit Miss Pee, not only because it was expected of us, but also because we were very thirsty and needed a drink of water. Miss Pee lived less than one block from the Cathedral, on the southern side of the church, in a very old and rather peculiar building. It was in fact a series of one-story buildings that were attached to each other along the sides. Each had only a front and back entrance. Some were family dwellings and others were business places. Because the buildings were attached along both sides, they were dark inside and there were many corridors. These corridors were long and narrow, as were the homes themselves. One could enter a building via a corridor and go all the way along the side of the dwelling to the back entrance. The bedrooms, living, and dining areas all opened to the single corridor that connected the front and back entrances. If the doors to the rooms were closed, one could walk right through a building via the corridor without ever intruding on a family or property owner.

When we arrived at the section of the series of structures that belonged to Miss Pee, her daughter-in-law, Miss June, was in her usual position at the front entrance of the corridor, hanging over the bottom half of the two-part door. With the top half of the door opened onto the sidewalk, she was engaged in her favorite pastime—watching people come and go in the busy neighborhood. Miss June was a pleasant, plump lady with a very light complexion. She knew us well, so as soon as we greeted her, she told us that Miss Pee was not in. When we asked Miss June for some water, she stepped aside and made room for us to pass. We hurried down the corridor past the closed doors that led to the home.

The home on the other side of these doors was much more interesting, we knew, than this dismal hall. There was one large bedroom and a long narrow room that was divided into two areas by the placement of furniture. There must have been a kitchen and there had to have been a place to dine, but I cannot find them in my memory. The rooms I do recall however are vivid.

In the bedroom there was a large canopied four poster bed of varnished wood. It was always well made with small dainty pillows tossed loosely towards the head of the bed. The bedspread was flowered with an eyelet design. It was a faded pink, but the flowers and green leaves saved it from too washed-out a look. The dainty pillows as well as the larger ones set against the headboard all had very lacy frills. There was only one side table on the left side of the bed which might have been better suited to an office than to this room. It was too tall, plain and very heavy and the color of the wood matched the wardrobe but not the bed. On this side table there were old photos in very ornate frames. The wardrobe was a rather masculine piece of furniture and seemed not to belong in this room either. In it there were a few dresses, and oddly enough, though no men lived there, there was a man's dark suit and a single dark green tie. I had seen Miss Pee open this often enough when we were visiting.

A large chest of drawers stood on the right of the bed. This was in yet a third shade of wood. There were two tiny drawers above the counter area, on either side of the large mirror where jewelry was stored; jewelry that was never worn. The lower level drawers had neatly folded items of clothing and the large drawers on the bottom contained household linens. All carried a very strong smell of camphor. The room was peopled with miniature ornaments all placed on lacy doilies. It was at once feminine and austere. The times that I had been called to that room to help Miss Pee find a shoe or zip up a dress, or sent to retrieve a shawl or book, I had been struck by the darkness of the room. It was an interesting but not inviting room.

The entrance to this room from the narrow corridor was permanently closed. The other entrance to the room was from the only other room I can recall. This was a miniature version of the drawing rooms in which I had imagined the ladies in the novels I read, served tea and crumpets to their friends.

The furniture here was elegant. All the pieces were straight backed, intricately designed, and wooden. The seats were upholstered in heavy brocade. The biggest chair could only accommodate two small persons, and there were many single chairs.

Just inside the other entrance to this room, the one from the long corridor, stood an imposing hat rack, a relic from an age when gentlemen wore hats. All the pictures that hung on the paneled walls in this room were faded black and white. In these photos, the women all wore high Victorian style collars, long dresses with long sleeves and sensible shoes. The men wore hats and carried canes. All the pictures seemed to have been taken indoors and all the subjects stood ramrod straight and stared directly into the camera. I was always struck by the fact that even the children managed to look morose as they peered thought their glass frames at the visitors below.

This room too had an ample share of miniature ornaments displayed on shelves, built into corners for just that purpose. There was a single window at the narrower end of the room, the only place that could accommodate a window. It looked out directly onto the sidewalk and was quite low. This window was only opened when someone was actually sitting at it, a deterrent to passersby who might otherwise gape into the room.

Halfway between the window and the entrance to the bedroom, a slim, tall well designed glass cabinet with a few pieces of valuable china sparsely arranged, stood as a divider in this long room. This second piece of the room contained the same type of furniture as the first, as indeed it was one room. This second area however was only used when there were enough guests to overflow from the main drawing room. This was also where Miss Pee sat to do some reading or sewing.

On this occasion, the inside of the house did not concern us; we went directly to the end of the corridor and out the back door to the tap in the yard. We cupped our hands to collect the water. After we had satisfied our thirst, we returned through the corridor, thanked Miss June for the water, and wished her a respectful farewell. On our arrival home, mom asked if we had visited Miss Pee. We said that we had stopped by to visit her, but that she had not been in and that was that . . . or so we thought.

Late that afternoon, Ma Lopice, perhaps not having Papa around to send over, shouted from her rocker to my mother to come over to take a telephone call. There was nothing unusual about this because we had no phone of our own and two neighbors allowed us to use their phone to make and receive calls. We used their telephones only in emergencies or at least for very important calls. When my mother returned from the call, she looked very upset. We assumed that there was bad news about my father's mother. These telephone calls were often about my aged grandmother, who gave the family a scare every now and then when ill health threatened to take her away from us. After taking the call, my mother did not say anything to any of us but went directly into her bedroom to my father. They spoke for a while and then my mother came out of the room and asked my brother and me to join them. This spelled trouble!

I was completely confused by this directive. I could think of nothing in the world that I could be in trouble for that would be initiated by a telephone call. My offenses were usually lo-cal—originating with my siblings or my mother. I also was not the kind of child whose wrongdoings ever needed to go to the high court—my father. My deeds were usually misdemeanors and were handled swiftly and effectively by the lower court—my mother. The only outside source that ever reported my misdeeds were my teachers, and it was usually scheduled. It came with my report card and the misdeed was always the same: "Marie talks too much in class." My academic performance was generally good and so even this complaint did not carry any penalty other than a verbal admonition not to talk in class. My brother, Allan, was even better behaved than I. He never talked in class. In fact, he barely spoke at home and he was never in trouble, not even in the lower court. So, it was confusing and even a little frightening for the two of us to be summoned together by both parents.

When we joined them in the bedroom, my father asked us to tell him exactly what had happened that morning when we went to visit Miss Pee. I was alarmed by his request. The visit had been a non-issue. Why would there be questions about it? I had noth-ing to hide, so despite my bewilderment, I reported what had happened that morning succinctly and accurately—we walked from the Cathedral to Miss Pee's home; we spoke with Miss June; we drank water; we said goodbye; we left. My father asked my brother if there was anything he wanted to add or change in my account. He confirmed the accuracy of my story. I could see my father's demeanor changing and I could tell he was getting agitated but somehow I did not think we were the cause of his upset. I did not feel that we were in trouble.

Despite the fact that my father appeared distant in his dealings with us and my mother was the one with whom we had most of our daily interaction, he seemed to really know and understand us better than my mother did. He knew who would do what and who would lie. He knew who was reliable and who was not. My mother, on the other hand, seemed always to be biased in favor of any adult. She seemed to accept the word of all adults over the word of any child, or at least any of her children. Sometimes she would not even give us an opportunity to defend ourselves against accusations, but would rather proceed to respond to the accusations as if they were indeed fact.

On one such occasion, my father had to take direct action to save Mark from trouble of this kind. A neighbor had come to complain that Mark had been teasing her daughter on the street. According to her story, Mark had accosted the girl who was at a standpipe and began to tease her. In the mother's account, her daughter had stood there innocently and had been victimized by my brother. By the end of the story, my mother was ready to punish Mark in front of the neighbor. Fortunately, my father had overheard the entire story from his place in the bedroom. When my father asked to speak with my mother quietly in the back, she knew she had to change plans. She dismissed the complainant with the assurance that the matter would be addressed. Mom went to the kitchen where she met my father waiting for her. There he informed her in what he thought were hushed tones, that his child was not to be punished based on those allegations. My father had observed the behavior of the girl in question—as well as the behavior of her mother—and though he knew that Mark was no saint, he did not believe the teasing was as unprovoked and one sided as reported. I believe this situation with Miss Pee was another one of these circumstances.

My father seemed satisfied with our explanation. He did not question us further, but directed Allan and me to get ready, and told my mother very firmly: "We are all going down there right now." When we were out of the room, I asked my mother why we were going to Miss Pee. She said that Miss Pee had been the person who had telephoned her, that she had been in a terrible rage, and said that my nine-year-old brother and I, then 10 years old, had broken into her Home. On hearing the charge, I got cold all over. My heart thumped in my chest and I felt as if I was going to choke. I had never even known of someone who broke into another person's place and now we were accused of doing this. We were being charged with burglary. I could not fully comprehend the charge. I asked my mother for more details, but she did not have much more to offer. Instead, she helped us to get ready quickly. I know from experience, with schoolmates and siblings, that in times of trouble each of the parties involved tries to represent the incidents in a way that favors their side without regard to accuracy. This however, was something new. That an adult would completely fabricate such a story and implicate two young children was outside of my experience.

Our drive to Marine Square took place in complete silence. My father continued to appear angry and to get more so as we drew nearer to our destination. It was difficult to define my mother's demeanor. When we arrived at Miss Pee's house, I was literally shivering. I was glad when my mother told us to remain in the car while she and my father went in. My father all but charged into the building with my mother following hurriedly in tow. After what seemed to us like forever, both my parents reappeared. We expected them to take us inside; instead, they got back into the car without a word to us and drove off. My father was controlled; my mother was quiet.

It seemed that my parents would not have said anything to us, but I was not going to allow them the luxury of silence. I wanted details. My mother reluctantly gave us a brief account of what transpired. Days later however, I deliberately eavesdropped as she explained in more detail to my aunt. She said that when they entered the house, they exchanged greetings briefly and perfunctorily. They asked to have Miss June present before they began to discuss the matter. After all, none of the three of them had been present at the time of the alleged offense. Miss Pee, for reasons unknown, tried to behave as if my parents' visit was a casual one. My guess is that she was surprised that they had come, and she knew that her daughter-in-law would know the truth. My parents suspected that Miss June had no idea what had brought them on that visit, and she was her usual pleasant self. She expressed pleasure at seeing them.

Once the greetings were over, strained as they were, my father asked Miss June directly to tell them everything she knew of our visit that morning. She appeared very surprised by the question as well as by my father's brusque tone. Not surprisingly, her account matched ours exactly. All turned now to Miss Pee for her response. They were unable to get her to repeat her accusation, apologize for it, or say why she had made it. In hindsight, Miss Pee may have had some neurosis or dementia, which had gone untreated. As well, she may just have been a mean-spirited old battle axe.

I believe my father would have cut her loose from the family after that incident, but my mother lived by the *seventy-times-seven* rule—the number of times one must forgive a person. So the next Sunday after 9:30 a.m. mass, Miss Pee was back in our home to spend the day, as if nothing had happened. But something had happened, and something would happen again. She had bigger fish to fry. Miss Pee had engaged four of the seven children in war. She had lost in each case. Now she was going for the chief. She was going after my dad.

Miss Pee's deceased husband had left her some property in a town called Claxton Bay. She wanted to sell this property. Now Claxton Bay was in the south of the island; we lived in the northwest and about 50 miles away from the property. My father hated driving and he relished spending his weekends reading in bed.

In spite of this, he assumed the role of driver/manager/realtor, whatever was needed. He drove every Saturday for many months to Claxton Bay to speak to potential buyers, to show the property, to do everything necessary to get the property sold. My dad was a reasonably kind man on his own, but I know it was his love and high regard for my mother that made him do as much as he did for Miss Pee. I know he was as eager as she was to get this property sold so that he could take back his weekends and limit the time he spent with this unpleasant old lady.

After many months of negotiating, there was a generous offer made, and the property was sold. Miss Pee had been a wizened old battle axe before, now she was a wizened old battle axe with money. We all hoped that this would be the end of our relationship with her, but we were wrong.

My father would have been comfortable dropping the Sunday routine because he thought now Miss Pee could use her money to find other ways to enjoy her day. I could sense that he was becoming less tolerant of her and even my mother had to work harder on him to keep allowing her to spend Sundays with us. My father was the only person in the family who drove, so if he did not pick her up she could not visit us. My father found it increasingly difficult to maintain the long established routine of picking her up at her home after 9:30 a.m. mass on Sundays. One Sunday, dad was "too sick" to go to mass, but surprisingly he was fine later in the day. Another week he went to mass but "forgot" to pick up Miss Pee afterwards. Unbelievably, after so many years of performing the same activity, his memory just failed him. Another Sunday dad went to mass, but "had to meet a friend after," and again could not get her. He came up with as many excuses as he could and we children were very grateful to him. Not surprisingly, we were happier on the Sundays that she was not around. We felt free. Even my parents talked to each other more and joked a lot.

I found out later that when the sale of the property was finalized, Miss Pee had offered my father some money as a sort of commission for the role he played. My dad had an unusually high sense of integrity and ethics, which did not allow him to accept the money. I believe one of the reasons for his refusal was to prevent Miss Pee from feeling she could use her money to influence or control him. Since he also wanted her out of our life, I imagine that he did not want to appear like an opportunist who had kept her around just long enough to get her money and then get rid of her.

My mother, who was more practical, considered that all the time away from his family, the wear and tear on his car, and the actual service of negotiating the sale, entitled him to the commission that Miss Pee had offered. My mother fully expected that Miss Pee would offer her the money my dad had earned and refused. Since my mother felt strongly about her position, my father agreed that because of the long family history and the close relationship my mother had with Miss Pee, which predated their marriage, he would not object to her accepting any monetary or other gifts offered to her by Miss Pee, as long as it was used for my mother's personal needs and not, under any circumstances, used for his children or his home. Well, it did not matter how my mother would have used the money or gift, because Miss Pee never offered her anything.

My father seemed convinced that Miss Pee's new financial circumstances would allow her to get along without our family. This was not the case and he grew resentful of her continued intrusion on the family. He had difficulty controlling his reaction when she drew attention to any of our infractions, which seemed a hobby of hers. He considered that we were sufficiently well disciplined and supervised not to require her intervention. In addition, he felt that she was an inconvenience to us. Sometimes she slept over and Lyn, Lul, or I had to give up our bed for her. Despite all that, she imposed on us without any effort to control her predisposition to complain and be annoying.

My mother never expressed any negative feelings toward Miss Pee. All who knew my mother would agree that she was a very good person. She was always striving to be better and treated everyone with respect and warmth. But no one had any strong evidence that my mother was deeply fond of Miss Pee. I believe that my mother treated her the way she did her 15-year-old pet dog, Bob. Bob could no longer hunt, fetch, protect anyone, or even control his bladder. He hardly barked and was slow and half blind. He got in mom's way as she chased around the house doing her chores, but instead of getting mad with him, she just moved around him and stopped often to pet him. Miss Pee, I think, was her 88-year-old human pet. Bob eventually had to be put to sleep and metaphorically, so did Miss Pee. Unlike Bob, her demise was neither swift nor painless.

Because of what happened, one might have concluded that Miss Pee was angry with my father for refusing the "commission" she offered him. It may have refuted her theory that he had been helping her, not out of kindness, but because he anticipated a reward. His refusal may have denied her the feeling of being entitled to throw her weight around our home. My father was a civil servant with a large family and her monetary offer had been significant. So, she may have considered that in refusing her money, my father was elevating himself or presenting himself as greater than she was. Whatever the reason, we did not know, but one cannot ignore the possibility that she may have been just a mean old bat. What we do know is that Miss Pee told a friend of hers that when the property in Claxton Bay was sold she had purchased a car for my father. This rumor was to say the least, not well received by my father when it reached his ears.

My father's desire was for immediate and brutal annihilation of the offender, from our family. My mother, ever the good Christian, was more contained. She was open to the possibility that such a rumor had originated with someone other than the accused. My mother suggested too that the person who gave the story to my dad may have been searching for information rather than actually reporting. It was hard for my mother to accept that this old lady would tell such a lie about people who had been nothing but good and kind to her. My father fully believed that she had made the statement, but he allowed himself to be contained. My mother's gentleness and love won my dad over, but not completely. There was a big part of him that wanted to let Miss Pee know what he thought of her and never to see her again. In the presence of Miss Pee, my dad became like a caged lion, and my mom a dedicated and skilled lion tamer.

In July 1960, when we moved to St. James, getting Ms. Pee on Sundays was definitely inconvenient. My dad stopped going to mass at the Cathedral and attended our new home parish. As a result, Miss Pee no longer came every Sunday, but she still came often. Any visit from her was too much for my dad and us children; it meant a lot to my mom, so it continued.

We had been in the new home a few months. It was Sunday, my family had just finished lunch and we were in bed for our usual Sunday afternoon nap, except for my parents who had stayed up to entertain Miss Pee. It was a warm day and my father and Miss Pee were having drinks while my mom sat at the table trying desperately to stay awake. She had prepared an elaborate lunch that day. She could not have known it then, but it was to be a farewell lunch for Miss Pee.

My mother, it seemed, let down her guard enough to let herself nod off at the table. She regained her composure but soon nodded off again. After nodding off for the third time, Miss Pee encouraged mom to go to her bed saying she would sit awhile with my dad and finish their brandies. That was her undoing. No sooner had my mother, the lion tamer, been out of earshot, that my father, the lion, saw his opportunity. He had consumed just enough brandy to relieve him of the inhibitions and social constraints that had allowed him to be polite in the past. His prey was cornered and defenseless. He began to roar and would not stop.

He had begun, I learned later, by casually informing Ms. Pee that a certain person had been saying that she had purchased a car for him. He said that this troubled him greatly since it was not true. Her nervous and evasive response instantly gave her away. Dad now had no doubt from her stammered response that she had indeed said such a thing. I believe, at that moment, he brought to bear all the rage, irritation and bad humor that he had contained so well for so many years. In clear, crisp, very curt language he told Miss Pee how dishonest, despicable, disagreeable, and vile a person she was. He sharply drew to her attention the fact that not even her sons or her only surviving daughter-in-law could endure her wickedness. My father's voice, by this time, raised well above his normal speaking voice, woke my mother who hurried to the dining room. One look at the situation and she knew she could not get the lion back in the cage. Instead, she hurriedly telephoned my uncle (called uncle but was actually a close friend and not a blood relative) and asked him to come and take Miss Pee home.

When my uncle got there, my father was shouting: "Get out! Get out! You old witch! My wife has been so good to you and this is what you do! You know you never gave this family a thing. All you did was take, take, take, and now you want to take my good name. Get out! Get out! And don't ever set foot in this house again!" The barrage of abuse confused Ms. Pee so much that when my uncle helped her into the car, she put her two feet on the seat and tried to sit on the top edge of the back seat. Her head hit the roof of the car and she had to be coaxed to put her feet on the floor and her bottom on the seat.

My siblings and I were very quiet when we awoke to my father's tirade. We stayed in our beds for all of it, as we knew that what was going on was not a setting for children. Some of us did get bold enough to follow as Auntie Missy was being led by my uncle and my mother, toward the car, and we were in the gallery watching boldly as she assumed the irregular position in the vehicle. We were silent through it all and even after. In fact, the entire household was as quiet as a church the rest of that Sunday. Much later, however, and for many decades thereafter, we would launch into peals of laughter when anyone mentioned or imitated how she got into the car that day. None of us I suspect, except maybe my mother, really regretted having her out of our lives.

Many months after her unplanned but very timely departure, Miss Pee was having a birthday. I know there was some discussion between my parents on the matter. I also know there was some disagreement between my parents on the subject. My mother, whether out of guilt, a sense of responsibility, genuine affection, or because of the early years she had shared with Miss Pee, was determined to acknowledge the birthday. I don't know why I was chosen to accompany her that night, but my mother seemed to have a connection with me that was not always in my best interest.

Anyway, with my father driving us in silence, we went off again to Marine Square to Miss Pee's quarters. We carried a gift, beautifully wrapped. My father remained in the car while my mother and I alighted. It was clear that we were not expected to stay long and that he would be waiting just where he was for us. When we neared the door, it was obvious that there were visitors in the house. The door from the street was opened for us by a guest who knew my mother and ushered us in. in the drawing room Miss Pee was in the middle of a small group of very old people and seemed to be telling a story. As we entered, she looked up and made eye contact, then averted her eyes and continued talking to her group. I was ready to run, but my mother with stoicism that is born of her good breeding, smiled broadly as if she had been warmly welcomed and approached the guest of honor. The guest of honor kept her eyes on her guests and tilted her head ever so slightly away from my mother as she approached to kiss her. She did not make any eye contact, nor did she look at the gift she was handed. She merely placed it on a small table nearby and continued giving her undivided attention to her other guests who now seemed to be less interested in the story being told and more interested in my mother—this less than welcomed guest. Someone offered my mother a chair, but all the fortitude in the world could not have withstood the coldness and insensitivity offered by Ms. Pee. I still recall the expression on my mother's face as she declined the seat and took her leave. Bravely, she maintained a facade of cheerfulness, stifling perhaps for my sake, her profound humiliation. We both hurried back to the car in quick measured steps. Even as we left, Miss Pee did not look in our direction.

My father sensed that it had been a bad experience and did not ask in my presence what had happened. My mother offered no explanation. Instead, it was her turn to sit in perfect silence all the way home. It was not the Sunday that Miss Pee was driven away from our home, but that birthday, that caused my mother to set aside for all time the relationship she had nurtured and protected for so many years.

Before she died, alone and penniless in a spare room of the house of a white expatriate who had relieved her of all of her money and her property, Miss Pee sent a message requesting to see my mother. My mother thanked the messenger and said, "Tell her you have delivered the message." Auntie Missy—Miss Pee—died some time later without having her request honored. I know of no one who truly mourned her passing.

Guilty By Reason of Gravy

*I*t was Sunday, notable for the lavish meals between noon and 1o'clock,e the popular family radio program of that time, "Auntie Kay", followed by the family's afternoon nap time. As an adult now, I suspect that my parents had initiated this quiet time with the children all in bed, because they had their own reasons for wanting to be in bed. Suffice to say, it was a time enjoyed by all.

Before retiring to the bedroom, my mother would put the food away. She put the meat—usually pork and chicken—in a cupboard, which she locked, taking the key to the bedroom with her. The rest of the food—callaloo, rice, ground provisions, macaroni pie, potato, vegetable salad, and plantains—was put in the refrigerator. The reason that the meat got singled out for special attention and placed under lock and key was because of another family tradition. On Mondays we had Pelau for lunch, our main meal of the day. This is a Trinidadian dish in which the rice and meat, and sometimes peas, are cooked together and served as one dish, generally just with a simple salad or slaw. The Pelau was made with meat that had been cooked on Sunday. The meat was not left over as such. It was deliberately done with Sunday's meat to make Monday's meal easier to prepare.

As a rule, no one got more than one serving of meat per meal. A second helping of the rest of the meal was available, but there was always only one helping of meat. Meat was not in great supply and there was little room for error. An extra piece given on Sunday might mean a piece short on Monday. Most of us understood and respected that. However, for a long time, meat had been mysteriously disappearing from the bowl in which it was put away on Sunday afternoon. This unsolved mystery led my mother to institute the lock and key system. Despite this precaution, meat still managed to vanish from the locked cupboard. With no real solution available, my mother carried on her futile efforts to secure the meat when she left the kitchen for Sunday afternoon nap.

This particular Sunday, Lyn must have had suspicions, because a subtle noise made by a careful thief in the kitchen could not have reached her in our bedroom, yet she got out of bed and went into the kitchen area. It may have been that she was on her way to the bathroom. Most homes in those days had only one bathroom and since it had to be accessible to guests as well as the family, it was located in the common area. Ours was just across from the end of the kitchen and at the end of the house near to the back door. Whatever took Lyn to the kitchen took her there just in time to catch my older brother, Elbert, in the act of stealing chicken from the dish in the cupboard, which had been securely locked by mom just minutes before and now was quite ajar. Her immediate response was a verbal exclamation and an open threat to report him to my parents. The thief tried immediately to deter her. Undaunted, she turned to go, intent on reporting the incident. My brother, knowing the trouble he would be facing when the report reached my parents, ran after Lyn offering bribes of every kind. He offered to do chores for her, do her homework, and made other meaningless promises. Lyn would not be stopped.

She walked hurriedly toward my parents' room, all the while calling him a thief. By the time they neared the bedroom, my mother had heard the chatter though she could not discern exactly what it was about and was already moving toward the bedroom door. Elbert heard the bolt move, knew the door was unlocked, and knowing that his game would be up, made a quick movement with the chicken leg which he still held in his hand, smearing the sweet gravy across Lyn's lips. When my mother opened the door she was faced with Lyn in front, lips dripping with gravy and Elbert behind, chicken leg in hand.

Lyn's momentary surprise at the chicken being passed over her lips caused her to pause just long enough for Elbert to steal her momentum and make a pre-emptive strike. He hastily and, might I say, very cunningly explained to my mother that both he and Lyn had been stealing meat, and because he refused to give her the leg that she wanted, she decided to report him. My mother, displeased at being made to leave her bed, fed up with one more case to resolve, and frustrated that there was no safe place to put the meat, did not allow Lyn any time to defend herself. After all, the guilt was written on her face in gravy. That was sufficient evidence. Mom declared that neither of them would have meat the next day and shut the door.

The case was never re-opened. The thief laughed. He had his Monday meat on Sunday; his punishment was just. He did the crime and was prepared to serve the penalty. Lyn, however, got no meat on Monday, had not got any extra on Sunday, and was denied the pleasure of getting someone in trouble. She also did not get any support from the rest of the siblings. She was always getting someone in trouble; this time it had backfired. Elbert told us the story the next day and has continued to tell it to relatives and friends all these decades since. It is always met with laughter and considered very funny. It was unfair; it was dishonest; it was even immoral and unjust; but it definitely was funny.

Auntie Bea

Miss Pee was only one of an assortment of older women who were part of my mother's childhood family circle, and remained attached to my mother to one degree or another. Some had fallen on hard times and came by when they wanted a nice home cooked meal, which they could always get at our home. Others were widowed and came by to enjoy the joy and warmth of our full house. Aside from Miss Pee, there was only one other person, Auntie Bea, who visited regularly. She did not come weekly or even monthly, but when she came she stayed for several days.

Unlike Miss Pee, Auntie Bea was a kind and well-meaning woman. Her husband had been a pharmacist and so she had led a comfortable life. She had no children of her own, but I had the impression that she had a long and happy marriage before her husband's sudden death. Although deceased as far back as I can remember, he must have been a remarkable husband to Auntie Bea and a close and dear friend to my parents. All three always spoke fondly of him. Auntie Bea's husband, Lenox, had been Lyn's

Godfather, and to be someone's Godfather was a special privilege. It was an honor bestowed on only very dear friends worthy of having such a distinguished role in the life of one's child.

Like Miss Pee, Auntie Bea was very inclined to see our faults and failings, or so it seemed to us. However, the two women could not have been more different. That difference was most pronounced in their physical appearance. Miss Pee was a sullen, shriveled up old woman who looked every bit her 88 years. She had small beady eyes that seemed to focus steadfastly on her prey. Her hair was unruly and dull in appearance. It would be misleading to say that she wore it short. The truth was that her hair barely covered her scalp and was resistant to all attempts at styling. It amused me to think that she was getting hair styling advice from the boy scouts that she led. Yes...she was a scout leader well into her 80s, and proud of it. Having an unending supply of children to provoke would have been appealing to her twisted mind.

Miss Pee's individual facial features were not unattractive, but together they did not create a face that was pleasing to the eye. I can only conclude that her inner ugliness masked any attractive physical attributes she may have had, at least to me. I don't recall that she ever smiled either, which would have given her face some relief from the sour expression she wore constantly. In stature, Miss Pee was barely, if at all, taller than the elementary school boy scouts that she led. She also shared chest size with them, breast included, and must have weighed about 100 pounds. What she lacked in stature, however, she made up with unpleasantness and wickedness.

I never gave Auntie Bea's looks much thought when she was alive, but in retrospect, she was a very pretty woman who must have been beautiful in her younger years. She was petite in stature also, but perhaps as much as 10 years younger than Miss Pee. She had light brown eyes and fine features that were noticeable because of her easy smile. Her round, rosy face was framed with thick wavy hair, which she wore in two braids wrapped into two disks on either side of her head just behind her ears. Her hair was so full that she never let it loose all at once. When grooming it, she would release only one braid at a time, straighten the part that divided her head in two, brush and comb through the loose hair, braid and rewrap that side before releasing the other braid. The first time I saw Auntie Bea combing her hair, I stopped and stared. I had never before seen a black woman with that much hair and I thought that combing it seemed a very big task for someone so small and old. Of course she managed it just fine. After all, she had owned that hair all of her life.

If you were a very early riser and you caught Auntie Bea in her night clothes, you would also catch sight of her braids falling loosely down her back or in front, on either side of her voluptuous breasts. Auntie Bea's breasts were so large on her small frame that they seemed to make her lean forward at an unnatural angle. Her breasts were never let free. Even under her night gown, Auntie Bea wore a kind of bedtime bra. It did not restrict and uplift her like a regular bra, but it did confine her breast enough to not flow all over the place, as I imagined they would, if left alone.

Auntie Bea was not nasty like Miss Pee. She was subtle in her fault finding, but did not seek to get us in trouble. She would always admonish us gently and she always had a proverb or adage to give us. She was always assigning us annoying little chores designed to reduce my mother's work load—always on the look-out to grab somebody to hang clothes on the line, clean up crumbs off the table, pick up paper off the floor, or clean a cloudy mirror in the bedroom. At mealtime no one wanted to be the first to ask to be excused from the table because, no matter how far away that person sat from Auntie Bea, that person would be detained and given an empty dish; my father's empty plate; something to carry away. No one was able to leave the table without taking something, in addition to his or her own plate, to the kitchen. It didn't matter how engrossed in conversation Auntie Bea may have appeared to be, we could never get away from the table without her input.

She tried to be helpful to my mother and often her helpfulness created more problems than it solved. I recall once when my mother had some clothes soaking in the washing machine, Auntie Bea observed that the machine was not full, so she went into our bedrooms and picked up some clothes to add to the load of soaking clothes. My mother had a quiet and controlled fit when she saw what had happened. The clothes in the washer were all white and had been soaking in detergent and chlorine bleach. The clothes that Auntie Bea added were colored and were completely destroyed by the bleach. Fortunately, the colors were not strong enough to ruin the white clothes in the washer. My mother never told Auntie Bea what her action had caused. She was just much more watchful of her when she was visiting.

Another time, Auntie Bea sweetened lemonade mom had been making to go with lunch. She wanted mom and the drink to get to the table more quickly. Maybe no one else stores salt in a large two pound jar, but we did. Unfortunately for Auntie Bea, we were unable to shield her from the consequences of that actions. The first person to taste the salted drink almost sprayed the entire table. My mother was quick to soften the embarrassment for Auntie Bea by saying she should have told her that we only use brown sugar and so anything white and granular was salt. The truth was that Auntie Bea never gave mom that chance, since she did not tell mom that she was going to sweeten the drink. My mother could not have stopped her from putting salt in the drink any more than she could have prevented her from adding two blue shirts, a yellow blouse, and a pair of striped pajamas to the bleach.

The most interesting thing about Auntie Bea, that was the source of a lot of mischief for us children, was that she was hard-of-hearing. She developed this problem well into her middle age so she never learned to lip-read. As children, we never knew her with good hearing. In my experience, people who have trouble hearing tend to speak loudly, not Auntie Bea. When she spoke to us, she generally made physical contact. She would touch our shoulder or arm and we had to stand still and lean in close to her to hear her when she spoke. We, in turn, had to shout to her, at least when we wanted her to hear us. There were numerous times when we would say things to her face that we knew she could not hear and which were designed to illicit laughter from others around. We would say these things always with smiles—as if we were saying something pleasant—and she, in turn, would smile right back at us. We would say: "Auntie Bea, you are very annoying. Do you know that?" or "Auntie Bea, we have had enough of you this visit. Don't you think it is time to go home?" Sometimes, we spoke to each other about her in her presence with comments like: "Isn't she a real pain in the ass?" or "You know, I think one day those breasts will make her lose her balance and fall on her face," to which the other person might answer: "At least she won't hear the *splat* when she hits the floor." We would even turn to include her, saying: "What do you think of that theory, Auntie Bea?" Her response was always a pleasant smile.

At mealtime she would ask everyone, as we approached our seat at the table, "Did you bathe your hands?" I don't know where she got that turn of phrase or why she felt that we still had to be told at every meal that we needed to wash our hands. She always asked us this, too, in a whisper. She was also very inclined to whisper things like: "All that glitters is not gold; a bird in the hand is worth two in the bush;" or "You never miss the water till the well runs dry." We all knew and understood these expressions, but she made them out of context and they seemed *a propos* of nothing. If we had listened to all that she whispered, she might have been unbearable, but we usually did not listen closely enough to be too bothered by the whispering.

My mother was always more than a little busy as she moved through the house doing her chores. She hardly ever stood still but when she did, it was for a very good reason. Allowing Auntie Bea to whisper to her was not a good reason. One day, I witnessed Auntie Bea stopping my mother in her busy tracks to whisper to her. This precipitated an unusual response from my mother.

She half listened for a few seconds and then with real irritability in her voice she did what we, the children, used to do. She said to Auntie Bea, at a pitch that Auntie Bea could not possibly hear, "Come on Bea, I have no time today for your secrets." My mother did not know that I witnessed this. She would have been embarrassed for me to see her behave this way. I also never shared this story with my siblings while we were growing up, but I was highly amused.

Auntie Bea passed away suddenly one day in Mid-March of 1965 while she was alone at home. She had been scheduled to visit us and had been hoping to move closer to us on a more permanent basis. My mother was devastated by her death and we were all sincerely saddened. We know that her love for my mother was genuine and was given with no restrictions. In fact, she expressed her feelings in a tangible way by leaving a substantial property for my mother. For a very short time it was rented and there were extra dollars to play with, but that period ended prematurely. Her entire estate, of which my father was the executor, incurred a considerable amount in death taxes and there was no cash with which to pay it. My parents decided to sell the property bequeathed to my mother to pay the taxes. There were numerous other beneficiaries to the will, but none of them understood the tax situation and had begun to make unsavory comments about our family when they had not received their bequests in a timely manner. My mother felt that her portion of the estate was not worth the loss of her family's good name and long-standing reputation. My father had always held the view that if one did not earn something by one's own sweat, then one had no claim to it. It was very easy, therefore, to dispose of the property to ensure that all the beneficiaries got what was coming to them. They got their gifts tax-free and my parents lost what was left to them. They put into practice, what so many people say about a gift: "It is the thought that counts." And it's true—Auntie Bea never had any thoughts but good ones toward us, and humor and childish pranks aside, we had nothing but good thoughts toward her as well.

The Bike

Generosity and true charity were very characteristic of my mother and expressed in everything she did with her family and everyone else. I believed one could tell that she was a wonderful person by just looking at her. Even her personal appearance reflected her personality. If I were to describe her with appropriate diplomacy for this period, I would say she was plump or somewhat overweight. The truth is...she was fat with an ample bosom and bouncing upper arms. She had a healthy head of short hair, which she kept brushed back under a hair net when she was at home. During the years of my childhood, it was not unfashionable for women to be seen wearing a hair net in public. My mother had delightfully brown eyes, and though her nose was—as I see it now—quite large for her face, it did not make her unattractive. The very large black mole on her nose got much more attention than her nose itself.

In every way, her personality matched the stereotype associated with her size. A very pleasant person with a very big heart, she was warm and affectionate and showed tremendous concern

for all. Everyone who stopped by our home received a warm welcome, and my mother always found some way to fill the needs
of everyone who needed her help. She always considered that
there was enough to share. Sometimes, when I observed her giving away things that I thought we could not afford to part with, I
would make a comment to her or question her recklessness. She
would say something to me about "casting your bread upon the
water and it will return to you . . ." In *my great wisdom*, I would
point out that the returned bread would be wet and of no use for
eating. My mother would always smile at me, at my humor, my
naivety, or my lack of understanding—I couldn't be sure. What
has stayed with me all these years, however, is the fact that she
always smiled when I made these remarks. We had this precise interaction more times than I can remember. In retrospect, I know
she was very right. We never missed whatever she gave away and
we never went without. In fact, I did not realize then how well
off we were, compared to many of our friends and neighbors. I
remember one particular occasion in which my mother's tender
heart caused even her otherwise understanding friends to think
she had gone too far.

We were living in Belmont and my older brother was accepted
into the high school of his choice—the school that both my parents very much wanted him to attend—although it was a far distance from our home. To make the commute easier for him, my
parents decided to buy my brother a bike. The cost of that bike
was quite considerable for my parents' income at that time and it
required tight financial planning to accommodate it into the budget. They did not buy it for cash. Instead, they made a down payment, and paid off the balance in monthly installments. The bike
was given to my brother as a Christmas gift, so in this way they
"killed two birds with one stone."

The bike was brand new and very shiny. It was also a man's
bike, which meant that it had a middle bar and was, therefore,
no temptation to us girls. My younger brothers had to be quite
persuasive to get my otherwise very agreeable and generous big

brother to allow them to ride his new bike. He considered them too young to be trusted with it and turned them down more often than he let them use it. My brother's friend, Jessie, on the other hand, was considered old enough and responsible enough to borrow his brand new bike.

Early one Saturday morning, Jessie borrowed the bike and rode off promising to return it later that day. The day wore on, and Jessie should have returned the bike, but he did not. The hours seemed to go by very slowly, and my brother began to be visibly worried. He walked to Jessie's home, but his family reported that Jessie was not there. When night fell and there was still no sign of either Jessie or the bike, my brother became very upset and began to panic. His distress was intensified because he had not told my parents that he was lending the bike to Jessie. Despite several more trips to Jessie's home, there was no bike and no Jessie. Saturday came to an end and the bike had not been returned. My poor brother got no sleep.

Early the next morning, he walked up the street again to Jessie's home. This time Jessie was at home, but there was no bike. Jessie's story was that he had gone to the race track, parked the bike and when he returned the bike was gone. It took my brother hours to make the five minute walk home with the news of the lost bike.

Both my parents were very angry and made no effort to hide their feelings. However, while my mother felt there had to be some way to recover the bike or its value from Jessie's family, my father's reasoning was that since he had done his duty as a parent to provide transportation for my brother to get to school, he no longer had any responsibility in that area; my brother needed to solve the problem he had created; and if necessary, he would have to walk the more than four miles—one way—to school. My father, having given his position on the matter, proceeded as if the issue was resolved. He totally separated himself from the problem and was contented. He considered the situation an apt consequence of my brother's choice and one he had to deal with alone.

After mulling over the problem for some time, my mother decided to visit Jessie's family. She firmly believed that the family had to accept responsibility for their child's carelessness and disregard for other people's property. She fully intended to let Jessie's parents know that she expected them to replace the bike and to do so before the start of the school term. My mother left for Jessie's home and was gone for a long time. Our anticipation was great and our anxieties even greater with each passing hour.

I don't have a clear recollection of how exactly my mother explained herself when she returned. She did not have the bike or any promise of a bike, yet she did not consider her mission unsuccessful. What we all vividly recall is that two days after my mother's initial visit to Jessie's parents, she returned to their home armed with an old sewing machine and two bags of groceries. Someone had to accompany her to help her carry these heavy items. It seemed Jessie's mother had been welcoming to my mother and had been very apologetic for Jessie's behavior and the loss of the bike. Jessie's mother disclosed that her son's behavior was becoming a problem and that it was quite possible that he might have sold the bike and not lost it, as he claimed. Jessie's parents had more children than they could support; and according to his mother, her husband could barely keep a job that paid enough to keep the family from starvation. Jessie's mother explained that she was able and willing to help earn an income to help the family finances, and was a competent seamstress, but did not have the capital required to purchase a sewing machine. It is not known whether my mother agreed to lend or to give the sewing machine to Jessie's mother, but we never saw it again. The bike was never mentioned again either, and my brother had to find his way to school on his own. Sometimes he got a ride with friends who, by then, all knew his predicament. Sometimes he took the not too reliable public transportation, for which he paid with his own money.

Fortunately, his problem did not last for a very long time. It seemed only a few months after the loss or bike sale incident that our family moved to the new home in St James, which was less than half a mile from my brother's school and an easy walk for him. Jessie, not surprisingly, ceased to be a friend after that bike incident. He did not do very well in school himself, and never held a proper job as an adult. After my mother's visit with Jessie's mother, there was never any direct contact between Jessie's family and ours, so we do not know if his mother ever made a success of herself as a seamstress with the donated sewing machine. My brother continued to be a very trusting person, which I guess is his nature, but fortunately he was never betrayed by anyone again as he was by Jessie on that early Saturday morning.

The Friendly Thief

In 1959, forty dollars could buy groceries for one week for my family of nine—seven children and two adults. It is difficult, therefore, to explain how much candy and goodies it could buy for children between the ages of six and nine. Candy was especially cheap, if one bought from the little store in Belmont known to all as "Hands Up." There, you could get five pieces of candy, each the size of a marble, for one cent. They came in different colors and flavors—all delicious. There was a bright orange, a bright green, blood red, and an amber color. Mints were about three times the size of these bright pretty colored candies and were sold two for one cent. My favorite by far was one of the most expensive pieces of candy in the store. It was a small block called a butternut. It was a rich flaky candy with pieces of peanuts hidden between the flakes. It had the overall flavor of peanut butter. That candy would run you a whole penny (two cents), but was well worth the cost. Five cents a week, therefore, would buy any child enough candy in any combination they chose. We were privileged to live very close to this store and we patronized it as often as funds would allow.

One Wednesday, during the Christmas school vacation, Robert came to spend the day with us. He was nine years old. His mother, Lola, was a single parent who worked as a store clerk and supplemented her income by sewing clothes for people. Ready-made clothes were not easily available, and when they were, they were costly and the quality was not particularly good. It was customary for people to employ the services of a seamstress for most of their clothing needs. Lola was always working at her sewing trade. She did this after her work in the store; after taking care of the needs of her children, and after they were in bed; and on Sundays. The store closed at 4 p.m. during the week and at noon on Saturdays. During the weeks before Christmas, however, the stores would remain open as late as 8 p.m. during the week, and up to 1 p.m. on Saturdays. The merchants wanted to give the working public every opportunity to spend every hard earned dollar in preparation for Christmas. Since my mother was a homemaker, formerly "housewife," she was always able to assist Lola by taking care of Robert when Lola went to work. During the school vacations, Robert would come to our house—sometimes every day. He was the youngest of four children. The first two boys were old enough to take jobs during the school vacation and usually did so. They always took jobs during Christmas, and this was a financial help to the family. The third child, Mavis, was in her mid-teens. While Lola worked, Mavis was cared for by a neighbor who had only one child, a girl. The girl and Mavis were the same age as well as close friends. Mavis spent a great deal of time at that home, and Lola was comfortable that all of her children were safe while she was at work.

Robert was close in age to my younger brother Allan, but he was not an easy boy to befriend. He was exceedingly restless. He never stayed still for long, did not seem interested in most games, did not play well with others, and spun some elaborate tales, which he tried to make us believe. Because his tales were so grand and so frequently told, it was difficult to take anything Robert said seriously. So, on that Wednesday in December, when he asked us to just say whatever kind of candy we wanted and he would get it for us, we dismissed him. When he insisted, however, we gave him requests for the most expensive candy in the store, just to shut him up. When Robert came back from the store with everyone's elaborate orders filled, we were stunned. We looked at the parade of candy blanketing the table and gasped. At first, no one dared to touch them. We could not imagine how Robert had been able to purchase all of that candy. When we insisted on knowing where he got the money for the candy, he spun a tale too extravagant to believe under normal circumstances. But when he showed us the ten dollar bill and the two single dollars that he had as change from a twenty, we were confused. We could not accept his story, but we saw that he did have money so at least he had not stolen the candy. We cautiously took the candy that was our individual order, but even so we were not eager to eat it. Something didn't seem right and we were worried.

A ten dollar bill was not something that any normal child ever owned. Children were not even given that much money to shop for groceries for their families, as the items would have been too numerous and too heavy to transport on foot. When our aunts, who saw us only a few times a year, generously gave us money to share among the seven of us, it never amounted to more than one dollar per child. Often it was five dollars to share among seven; that amount was a delight and it gave us a range of choices as to how to spend it. We had seen Robert's twelve dollars in change; we had seen the eight dollars' worth of candy; we were very confused.

Before the end of that day Robert was taking requests again, this time for toys. By now we were excited and no longer too concerned about the source of the money, preferring instead to think carefully about the toys we would request. We wanted to ask for things we really wanted, because now we believed Robert would deliver. We were willing to benefit from Robert's largess, but neither Allan nor Mark was willing to go to the store with Robert for the purchases. Deep down, I guess we did not trust Robert or his tales and we were not willing to step out in public with him and his money.

The first time Robert asked mom's permission to go to the candy store, she thought nothing of it. He had already had lunch and there was no risk of spoiling his appetite. So if, as he said, his mother had given him money to buy candy, there seemed no reason to object. The store was only a few yards away from our home. My mother never saw the tabletop full of candy with which he returned because she had been busy in the yard, hanging clothes out to dry. When Robert asked to go farther up the street, she hesitated, but he told her that he wanted to use the money his mother had given to him for candy, to buy a roll of caps for his toy gun. A roll of caps cost five cents so that would fit whatever his mother might have given him, and the request did not seem unreasonable. Robert was at the age where boys played with guns and caps all the time, and in those days, it was entirely safe for a child of nine to walk to the corner store alone.

Robert returned with 15 rolls of caps, five for each of my brothers, Allan and Mark, and five for himself. My oldest and youngest brothers did not share in this. In addition, he had purchased three brand new toy guns in which to use the caps. Again, there was one for each of the boys and one for him. He apologized for not filling my order but promised that he would do so the next day, as he said he had more money at home. My brothers' toys did not serve them very well, because though Robert was able to play with his caps and gun, my brothers were not. Since Robert had asked mom to allow him to go to buy caps, mom would assume that he had a gun, which he brought from home. On the other hand, she knew that my brothers did not own such toys. The last time they got new toys had been at Christmas, and after eleven months those toys either did not exist or were not in working order. My mother knew what toys her children owned and their source. My brothers knew instinctively that they could not give my mother the complicated story that Robert had given to us about how he had come by that large amount of money—a story that changed as the day progressed.

Robert had told me that his father, who had been separated from his mother since Robert was six years old, had remained in touch with him. According to Robert, his father secretly visited him at school on a regular basis and always gave him money and other gifts. It was known, even to us kids, that Lola struggled financially because her estranged husband had refused to give her one penny unless she allowed him to come back and live in the home with her and the children, and she would not consider that. Her husband had been known to be physically abusive to her and her daughter and so for Lola, reconciliation was not an option. Robert said that his father gave him money regularly but told him to keep it a secret from his mother.

Robert's story to one of my brothers was markedly different. He maintained that he had found a wad of money in the school yard on the last day of school. He said he did not tell his mother about it because she would make him take it to the police station. My brother asked him how it was that he had not spent any of it since he had found it more than a week before. First, he said that he was waiting to share it with friends like us because he did not want to share it with people who would want to take it from him. At another time he said that he had indeed been spending it, but that it was quite a lot of money so there was still a lot left. We knew that none of what he said was true, but we ate our candy and my brothers accepted their guns and caps and hid them hoping to find an opportunity to play with them without being seen by my mother.

Caps are little paper discs that house an explosive substance. They were sold in small rolls or spools. The explosive part was a raised disc with a coating similar to the head of a match positioned on narrow strips of paper, each disc just a fraction of an inch away from the other. When these discs were hit with a stone or heavy metal object, they would create a minor explosion, sometimes with a tiny spark of fire, and the pungent scent of burned sulfur.

Strictly speaking, one did not need a gun to use the caps, but it was just a lot more fun firing the caps with a gun. This was a relatively simple operation. The roll of caps was placed on a spindle located inside the chamber of the gun, then about ¼ of an inch of the lose end of the roll was drawn out and placed under the hammer of the gun. When the trigger was pulled, the hammer would be activated to slide back and then come down forcefully on the disc of the cap. Each hit with the hammer would set off the explosion and turn the spool, releasing more of the caps to the hammer. Young boys of the time had great fun with these guns. They delighted in playing *Cowboys and Indians* using these guns. If there was only one gun, then the cowboy would shoot the un-armed Indian as demonstrated in American movies depicting confrontations between these groups. If there was more than one gun, the cowboys took the game outside a salon for a drawdown and shootout. Since children spent most of their leisure time outside, these shooting wars could go on intermittently all day during the school vacation. While Robert was around, my brothers took turns using his gun to set off their caps. When he left, however, they had to be content with hitting the caps on the ground with a stone. They could not be found by my mother using the guns that Robert purchased.

On Thursday, Lola brought Robert by early. She did not start at the store until mid-morning, but she was going to be working late. She stayed a while talking to my mother and even shared what was left of our breakfast. While the two women were eating, Robert sneaked out of the house—without being missed by anyone—and by the time his mother was ready to leave for work, he had already procured the items he had promised Lul and me the day before. Lyn was too old to play with us, and we would never have involved her in these shady arrangements anyway because she was such a tattletale. Robert bought us little plastic tea sets, jump ropes, a game of jacks, and he even bought a jigsaw puzzle for no one in particular. He still had more than five dollars left at the end of the second day, despite treating us all to popsicles, when the ice cream cart rolled by. My mother gave us a squinted look when we told her that Robert had paid for our treats. The total was only 25 cents, so she let it go. She probably decided that Lola was indulging Robert a bit since she had to be away from him so much. She might also have been impressed with Robert's generosity.

Before Robert left late that evening, he said that he would have more surprises for us the next day, Friday. Frankly we were already quite satiated. All of our needs had always been met by our parents and our wants were few. A ton of candy, new toys, and popsicles had been more than enough for us all. Sadly, despite the gifts, we did not really like Robert any more than we had before he had turned into Santa Claus. We found him still difficult to play with and we did not trust him. His lavish gifts only intensified that mistrust and in the last two days, too much time and attention had been given over to his money and his lies. We decided that Friday there would be no more gifts, no more candy. We would go back to our normal, safe, predictable lives.

That night after dinner, my parents retired to their room, and we to ours. Lul and I played with our jacks and my older sister was trying to sleep when we became aware of our parents arguing in the next room. At first, we paid no heed to it, but it got louder. We listened as my father stopped talking and my mother left the room. When she returned, we heard the rustle of papers and my mother's voice saying, "Look, see for yourself." My father responded, "I don't care what you have written there, you count for yourself." Then my mother, "I don't want to count it again. I am showing you what I spent. I am not crazy." They were now quarrelling so loudly and for so long that we could not concentrate on our game even if we wanted to. Lul was only five and she did not care to listen to my parents quarrel so she took her doll and tea set, sat on the floor, and entered the imaginary place where she had tea with her dolls and they enjoyed each other's company. My older sister, Lyn, could not possibly have been asleep as she wanted us to believe, but I did not care about her pretending.

I was interested in what was going on in the next room and I was listening intently.

The argument had been going on longer than any I had over-head, and it didn't seem to be going anywhere. The topic was very narrow and each party just kept repeating their points. As it went on, I finally got the gist of the discontent. My mother had gone shopping on Tuesday, for Christmas gifts. She had a detailed account of all that she had spent on each gift. On Wednesday evening there had been a discrepancy between what she said she had spent and the money left in the "account." The difference was twenty dollars. My mother had been sure of her figures, but could not dispute my father's claim that the money missing was more than she said she had spent. This argument seemed to be a continuation of the night before except that this evening there was an additional twenty dollars short in the "account" and mom had not left the house and had no opportunity to spend money. There was no question that my father had spent any money since he never did any shopping of any kind. He did not even buy his own shoes. He was also able to show cash left from the last time he had taken money, which had been several days before...before my mother had gone shopping, and before the first twenty dollars had been missing.

My parents had a very simple and practical banking system, and only one active "account." When my father got his monthly pay it was brought home in cash and rolled up and put in the top right hand drawer of the dresser in their bedroom. Before it was put in the drawer, my father took out his spending money that had been agreed upon in their budget. The groceries and vegetable market cost was a set amount every week. Mom would roll this out and keep it in a separate place to use as she purchased the items needed. When my mother needed other money for house-hold expenses or for items for the children, she would take it from the drawer and make a note of the money taken and how it was spent. As responsible people, with a fixed limited income and sev-en children, my parents were very organized about spending.

On Wednesday evening, my mom had gone to the "account" for some reason and found that it was short by twenty dollars. She asked dad about it. He knew nothing about it. Each one of them had accused the other of being the one responsible for the deficit. Dad suggested first that mom had purchased something that she had not written down and had forgotten about. Whenever there was an expenditure that had not been pre-arranged, the cost of this was written in a notebook which was also kept in the drawer with the money. Even though mom had insisted that all the money she had taken for Christmas shopping had been accounted for, there remained lurking in her mind the possibility, slim though it was, that two notes had stuck together when she had counted them out, and remained stuck when they were spent. That was my father's final theory, and there was no evidence to the contrary. Both agreed, however, that there was twenty dollars short on Wednesday evening. When on Thursday night, with no spending activity by either adult that day, the balance in the drawer was yet another twenty dollars short, there had to be another answer. After a while the quarrel ended, but my parents continued to talk in soft, calm, friendly tones for a long time before I fell asleep.

The next morning very early, my parents summoned me and all of my siblings to their room. They asked us individually if any of us had taken any money from the drawer. That they kept money there was no secret to anyone in the family. Their particular banking system had been in place for years and there had never before been a problem—certainly not one of this magnitude. This was a huge setback. Forty dollars represented about ten percent of the total amount put in the drawer to see the family through an entire month. This was December and there were additional expenses for gifts and food. Everyone denied having ever been in the drawer. As children we had little reason to be in our parents' room unless we were there to talk to them, had been sent to fetch a specific item, or summoned, as was the case that morning. After all the denials, there were some more probing questions asked, which led to the disclosure that Robert had been known to have spent twenty dollars on Wednesday and another sizeable amount on Thursday.

That morning when Robert was dropped off, his mother did not come out of the car. She was being taken to work by a neighbor who dropped Robert off first. My parents would not have the opportunity to talk to her until the end of her shift that evening. By that time, they had easily and casually got a confession from Robert who unknowingly had repeated his actions of Wednesday and Thursday but this time under the watchful eyes of my parents who were poised and ready and caught him in the act of helping himself to another twenty dollar bill. Once he was caught, it was easy to get him to confess to the acts of the two days prior. To Robert, the day seemed to go on as usual. He was treated no differently than he had in the past. He had acknowledged to my parents that he knew what he had done, and that was all that happened until his mother arrived that evening.

Being the kind hearted person that my mother was, I think she was more upset about what the news would mean for Lola, than she was about what the loss meant to our family. She knew that my father would insist that the money be repaid and my mother knew what a difficult time Lola was already having making ends meet. Many days Lola had to give her family meals without meat. She could only afford a two bedroom house for the family of five; and to maintain even this lifestyle, she was up doing her sewing into the wee hours of the morning—even though she had a full day on her feet in the store the next day.

Whenever my mother looked at Robert, I could see sadness and worry in her eyes. Although he said he understood what he had done, Robert seemed unperturbed by the whole affair and was happily at play climbing the two small trees in our backyard and running from one end of the yard to the other at full speed— smiling and laughing as if he had won a race against others. He did not want to interact with us, nor we with him. It was difficult for us to imagine someone, let alone a nine-year-old, stealing forty dollars when we wouldn't pick up and keep a penny off the floor if we knew it had fallen out of dad's pocket or mom's purse. We felt ashamed that we were, albeit unwittingly, participants and beneficiaries of the crime. We voluntarily turned over all of our ill-gotten goods to our parents and told them as well about the candy we had consumed. That day seemed very long indeed and, unlike Robert, none of us was much inclined to play. We read and re-read our story books and were restless ourselves. Lola's arrival was tensely awaited.

She arrived late and tired from her very demanding job. We could tell that she wanted to just pick Robert up, get the bus, and head home. My mother indicated that there was something to talk about and she presented Lola with a plate of food in such a way that refusal was hardly an option. She took a long time in the kitchen getting a drink to go with the meal. While Lola ate, mom chattered rather than chatted with her. She went on about the back door hinge that was coming undone and the man who was to come to repair it, who had not shown up as he promised. She kept going in and out of the dining room, staying in just enough to keep Lola comfortable and out enough so that she would not betray anything. Whether in or out of the room she kept up the chatter, punctuated unnaturally with small laughs. Mom was clearly very uncomfortable.

Lola was tired and glad for a tasty home cooked meal and could not have suspected anything as awful as she was about to hear. Robert, for his part, had greeted his mother as usual and retreated to the middle bedroom where my younger sister, two of my younger brothers and I sat quietly waiting for the bomb to drop. Despite our obvious discomfort and tension, Robert proceeded to regale us with his fanciful accounts. He seemed to have a need to move about and to talk. Some of his stories involved acting out roles and using a different voice. Ordinarily we would at least have been amused by him. This evening we were just irritated and really craved silence. We did not want his noises to cause us to miss the moment when our parents broke the news to his mom. We could hear from the scraping of the cutlery against the plate that Lola was at the end of the meal. We also heard her complimenting my mother on the meal and thanking her for it. We knew the moment was near.

At this point, we would have moved closer to the door, which we already had opened ever so slightly, to allow for sound to travel, but there was no need. My mother pushed the door wide open and asked us all to go into the next bedroom immediately. She closed the door securely and we heard her ask Lola to join her in the living room. These two moves created so much distance between us and them that it was impossible to hear what anyone said. My father joined my mom and Lola in the living room and they began to speak. All spoke in calm quiet tones. Nothing could be understood even by those of us brave enough to occasionally sneak back into the middle bedroom on the pretense that we needed a book or a bookmark or a doll. At some point in the exchange, my mother came to the bedroom and asked Robert to go with her. The defendant was now in the courtroom. We could hear Lola speaking to him a little more loudly than she had been speaking with my parents. We could identify from her tone when a question was asked of him and we would hear the occasional "Answer me!" or "Don't shake your head, I want an answer *yes* or *no* right now!" Robert's voice could not be heard at all in the exchange. His time in the court was brief. I suppose once he established his plea, there was no further use for him. Not surprisingly, he came back into the bedroom with a big smile, as if he had just received an award. No one asked him anything. He lay down on the bed smiling up at the ceiling. The sentencing phase was short, and then Robert was called to go home. We were not called to say goodbye to Robert and Lola, but we presented ourselves anyway. Lola's eyes were swollen and red. It was clear that she had been crying. Her farewell was weak and distant. She looked mainly at her feet as she began to exit. As they approached the front door, my mother stopped Lola and handed her a bag into which she had just put the last of our newly purchased toys. Lola tried to wave it away and dismiss it with a shrug, but my mother insisted that she take it, suggesting weakly that Lola could wrap the items and give them as gifts for Christmas. She took the bag absently and moving in a robot-like trance she pushed Robert ahead of her as they headed for the bus stop. When mom turned to go back into the house, I saw that she too had been crying. I am not sure why, but I was very sad as well and had to wipe away a tear or two of my own.

The rest of that evening the house was quiet as a church, or as church used to be back then. My mother took longer than usual with the dishes and she did not ask me to help. She scrubbed the counter tops with a brush and cleaned out one of the cupboards and repapered the floor of that cupboard. Later that night, she repacked the cupboard. It may have been a routine task for that period just before Christmas, but the activity just stood out for me that night. My father too did not return to his bed but sat in the living room reading that day's paper, which I was sure he had done earlier that day. My siblings and I talked a lot about Robert and wondered aloud whether he would be with us again next day. Before we went to bed we had the answer. My mother came into the room and announced, "Robert will no longer be staying with us during the week. Girls go into your own room now and it is time for everyone to go to sleep." She left the room, and in complete silence we did as we were told.

My older brother and sister, in my recollection of this story, seem to have been non-existent though I know they must have been somewhere. It strikes me as odd that we were able to get away with the candy and the toys without Lyn telling mom on us. It seemed that her main role in the family was to tell tales that would get us in trouble and to always be in a place to "overhear" adult conversation. It was her second talent that got us the conclusion of the Robert story. We found out what happened in the penalty phase. My sister "happened to overhear" my mother telling my aunt, that since Lola had no means to repay the debt in cash, it was agreed that she would meet the obligation of the debt through her profession as a seamstress. She used to make clothes for us anyway and would continue to do so except now the charge for her services would be offset against the debt until it had been repaid in full.

That arrangement was considerate and sensitive on the part of my parents, but I wondered how practical it was. I wondered how long it would be before that debt would be paid. We only had new dresses made at Christmas and white dresses made in January when, just before her birthday on January 19th every year, my grandmother would come close to dying. Then she would rally, celebrate her birthday, and be in good health again until next January. I recall this happening from the time I was eight years old. When she did die at the age of ninety-five I was working, bought my own dress from a store in Manhattan, it was not white, and I flew in from New York, where I was living, to attend the funeral. She did die in January, but it was after her birthday, on January 29, 1971. As luck would have it though, the January after Lola's plea deal, my grandmother did not attempt to die. Our Christmas dresses for that year were already made and paid for before Robert's offense, so the full debt would have to hang over Lola for a year before she would be able to start reducing it with Christmas dresses for 1960. By that time however, we were in our new neighborhood, Lola's financial situation had become dire and she had been evicted from the two bedroom house that she was renting. Contact with our family now was minimal. It is unlikely that she ever was able to "work off" much, if any, of that debt. My parents got a new, safer accounting system which involved a check book and frequent trips to the bank.

The Christmas Pig

*I*n the days of which I write, Trinidad was predominantly a Christian nation and Christmas was a very important celebration. We had special music called Parang, a remnant of our Spanish heritage, and distinctive foods and customs that were unique to our twin island nation.

Christmas was the only time of the year that imported fruits such as apples, grapes, and pears were available. These fruits were quite expensive, but an absolute delight during the holiday season. My family usually partnered with another family to purchase a crate of apples. Our share was 24 apples, which my mother served sparingly throughout the holidays. No one got more than one half of an apple per serving, and often we got just one quarter. At that rate, and because they were not refrigerated, by the time mom got to the last ones at the bottom of the crate, they had begun to rot.

As Christmas approached, just the smell of apples was cause for celebration and the street vendors' displays were a feast to the eyes of a child. I felt happy just being in the midst of this commerce. I enjoyed being among the throngs of people moving along the sidewalks and in the streets, and bustling between slow moving cars as they crossed from one side of the street to the other.

The street vendors had portable stalls that were really large box carts set on wheels, which allowed them to move their carts during the course of the day if a more favorable location became available. Setting the carts on wheels also allowed the vendors to relocate quickly if rain threatened to soak them or their produce. Vendors were almost always women—fat women in colorful cotton print dresses with full skirts and large pockets, where they kept their money without any fear of being robbed. They chatted comfortably with each other and with the customers, leisurely navigating the narrow divide between social interaction and business transaction. There would be questions about each other's children or husbands, if the customer was a "regular." There would be little exchanges about Christmas shopping; children being out of school, on vacation; the expenses coming after Christmas with the return to school and the need for new uniforms and shoes.

Children always grew during the vacation, even short Christmas vacations. They had mini growth spurts in December and they blossomed fully during the "August vacation" (from early July to early September). This period has now been renamed "summer vacation." Since its summer year-round in Trinidad, it seems silly to me to adopt this term...but in keeping with the acculturation to all things American, challenging its usage is an exercise in futility and I am forced to surrender my point and focus on growth spurts. All school children, in pre-schools, primary schools, and secondary schools, wore uniforms, so their growth, during the vacations, presented a significant cost to parents just before schools re-opened in January. These conversations between the vendors and their customers took longer than the sale transaction and often delayed the next customer in line, but no one minded. There would even be jokes exchanged between the customers and vendors and it was okay for one to tease the other. People had a wonderful sense of humor and moved about with languid ease. No one ever seemed to be in a hurry about anything.

Along with the apples at Christmas, we also had boxed chocolates—an assortment of little brown chocolates, with cool sweet sticky surprises inside. I preferred those with nuts inside but, they were all sweet mysteries since no one ever knew what filling was inside which piece of chocolate. Christmas cookies came in very attractive round tins, which, when fully relieved of their contents, became cake tins for the next season's baking. We called the cookies *biscuits*, and there were sweet biscuits and salt biscuits. The salt biscuits are now more commonly called crackers. The sweet biscuits, like the chocolates, had different shapes. Some were heart-shaped; some were square; some were oblong; and some were shaped like pretzels—a term no one knew at that time and not an item one would find in shops in Trinidad even today. Some of the sweet biscuits had a white creamy filling; others had a substance like dried-up jam holding the top and bottom of the biscuits together.

During the days leading up to Christmas, and after school had been closed for the month—mid-December to mid-January—the house was a hive of activity. We changed all the curtains and re-covered all the cushions in the house. The wood furniture and floors were stripped, sanded, and varnished. The steps and walkway leading up to the house were given a fresh coat of red paint, in keeping with all the other red steps that could be seen near and far. The banisters, the walls outside the house, and the porch chairs all got a new coat of paint. Old picture frames were redone with shiny gold paint. The cutlery was reminded that it was real silver and its luster was allowed to shine after a good coating of polish and a hard shine with newspaper. The large brass vases in the living room and porch were blinding once their brilliance was restored with Brasso (the only product of its kind at the time), and powerfully buffed and shined with newspaper. Their dented areas were turned away from view of visitors and they were filled with tacky, unnaturally colored plastic flowers imported from China and sold at a grand store called Excellent Trading. Silk flowers or any flowers that approximated the look of real flowers were still in the future.

Before baking began, all the kitchen cupboards had to be emptied completely; the contents washed and dried; and the cupboard itself scrubbed and left to dry. Before returning the items to the cupboard, the shelves in the cupboard were covered with paper that was not always cut to size. The items were then replaced on the shelves in order of height, with all the labels facing out. The top shelves were done first, then the bottom ones. The bottom shelves were very deep and it was not uncommon to find spiders and webs, as well as a dead roach or two in the darker recesses of those cupboard shelves. Those deep shelves were home to baking pans, old biscuit tins, regular pots and very large bottles of oil, and gasoline. Yes, gasoline was kept in the kitchen.

The top cupboard doors were all made of glass and they were spotless by Christmas day. The open shelves, at the top end of the row of cupboards, were painted white. This exposed area of cupboard shelves is where we put decorative knick knacks. The real purpose of this space, however, was a kind of medicine cabinet without doors. These shelves held items that one would normally have in a bathroom today. But in my house those things like: cough syrup, Band-Aids, Dettol (an antiseptic lotion), Vaseline, aspirin, Limacol Mentholated (a skin coolant and headache reliever), even new boxes of toothpaste, and bars of soap, found their way onto those shelves. Before long, the decorative items at the front often got broken or mixed in with more useful items at the back.

The kitchen had the only non-wood flooring in the house. Using a small brush, we painstakingly cleaned the grout between the ceramic tiles. We even moved the refrigerator and stove to clean the tiles under them as well, and we applied the same meticulous care to both appliances.

We made as many changes with the furniture as the space would allow. One year, I recall, that after exploring several options in the living room, we found that we just could not place the piano. Determined to move things around and create a new look, we carried the piano outside, never to return it to any place inside the house. The big, heavy, ugly black creature, its white teeth exposed occasionally when the neighbors came over to play with us, remained in the backyard until a man came and took it away. The man dealt in musical instruments and had tuned that piano for us many times before, when it lived inside the house. By the time the piano was put out of the house, everyone had come to accept that no musician would come from our family. Lyn and I had taken music lessons for years, but had no affinity for it. We had to be reminded all the time to practice; we never did it on our own. It was, for me, just one more chore to do and *to get over with*. The piano was literally just taking up valuable space in the living room and when it was finally removed, its absence went unnoticed.

By Christmas Eve, we were done with most of the heavier work. All the paint and varnish had dried. We had to hang the curtains, which was an easy task. They were held in place with spring rods attached by screws to a hook in the wall. It was just a matter of putting the screw on one end of the rod unto one hook and then stretching the rod so that the screw at the other end would reach the second hook. Then, we spread the folds of the fabric along the rod as evenly as possible from one end to next.

New doilies were placed under every vase and ashtray, and the plastic flowers were arranged as well as they could be. Last minute touches were given to the display glass in a special cabinet that was the guardian of the "good glassware." Some of them were wedding gifts; others were of great sentimental value, passed down from my mother's parents, Pa and Nen, long deceased by then. The glassware had been washed and dried already by me—the only child careful and trustworthy enough for such a task—put back in the cabinet with utmost care, and glistening for all to see.

At the same time, the ham was cooking in a large, commercial-sized pan that originally housed cooking oil. The oil was bottled on the premises of the shop that sold it. As a rule, patrons, purchasing oil, walked with their own bottles. They were often bottles that previously held rum or some other form of alcohol. The tin, in which the ham was cooked, was often picked up free of charge from the grocer. The grocer gave them away to the patrons who asked, once the tins were emptied of their contents.

My family always went to my grandmother's for Christmas, so my mother did not prepare a Christmas meal. She did, however, prepare a meal just as grand as the Christmas meal, the day after Christmas when my parents entertained the entire extended family and celebrated their wedding anniversary. Turkey and pork were the big meats on this day. Turkey was imported and available in the large supermarkets. Pork, in the large amounts that we needed, was purchased directly from the butcher. It was usually ordered weeks, sometimes months, before Christmas. Meats were all marinated before Christmas day (and left in the refrigerator) to be cooked on Boxing Day.

One year, right after Christmas, my father came up with a great plan. A young pig was cheap to buy and feed. It also grew fast; so a pig, bought early in the year, would be the perfect size by Christmas. My father had a friend, Neville, who was an essential part of this plan. Neville and my father were close friends when they were young boys in elementary school, in one of the smaller towns in a semi-rural area. After they had received all of the education available to them in their hometown, Neville engaged in farming on his small family compound, while my father joined a pharmacist as an apprentice in the same town. Both remained close friends.

At some point in his training to become a pharmacist, the person to whom my father was apprenticed, made an error in filling a prescription for one of the locals. The error proved fatal. The story spread quickly, as things do in small towns, from one drawing room to the next. There was a great outpouring of sympathy for the family of the victim and the pharmacist in question became infamous. This incident immediately convinced my grandmother that pharmacology was a risky profession for my father to pursue and she arranged for his apprenticeship to be terminated instantly.

Teaching had always been an honorable profession, so my grandmother was happy when my father decided to train instead to become a teacher. His older sister had already done so successfully and was teaching in a school in the neighborhood where the family lived and where she was very well respected. The first phase of the training was something of a mentorship program, and he did this close to home. After about one year, he was required to relocate to the city of Port-of-Spain to embark on more years of training at the only teacher training college on the island. The actual distance by road today, from Port-of-Spain to my father's family home, is less than 40 miles. However, in the late 1920s to early 1930s, with limited transportation and communication, the two places might as well have been an ocean apart. Dad's visits home were only during vacations and on holidays. As a result of this extended stay on campus and participation in campus life, he began to form strong bonds with the people with whom he studied and lived. There was a distance being naturally created between himself and his boyhood friend Neville. In addition, though my dad still identified with his small town and cherished Neville as a dear friend, Neville's insecurities began to surface and together these factors stunted the growth of the friendship.

By the time my father married and had his family, he was living in the city exclusively. Going home for him was something he did only a few times a year, when we all went to visit our grandmother. By the time I knew of Neville, decades had elapsed since the days when he enjoyed a really close friendship with my father. Neville also had a family of his own now. He had married a girl from the area and they had two daughters. On some occasions, when we visited my grandmother and spinster aunts (all of whom still lived in the family home), my dad would go off to check on the people and places of his youth. Neville was always one of the people he visited and from all accounts, Neville was always happy to see him. Neville however never came to visit dad, not at my grandmother's or at our home in Port-of-Spain.

My father was not happy that his old friend did not know his family, so one afternoon when we were visiting my grandmother, I was not yet a teen, my father packed five of us into the car and took the short ride to Neville's home. Telephones were not very common among regular folk yet, so Neville had not been warned or prepared for our visit.

Neville was living primarily off the land, so he was often in the field, and Sunday was no exception. When my father parked the car in the large yard and started toward Neville's house, an attractive, buxom woman with a round face and a very sincere smile came out to greet us. She had a full head of thick black hair, which had not been processed in any way. It was in its natural state and because there was so much of it, her head had the appearance of being too large for her body. This woman and my dad held each other in a long, warm embrace all the while exchanging compliments. When my father introduced us to her, she encircled us individually in a similar embrace. Before she ushered us into the house, she called out to a young man who had been unselfconsciously hanging over the fence from the adjoining property, taking in every aspect of our approach and greeting. She sent him off to get Neville who was tending to the animals in a far corner of the farm.

The neighborhood messenger did not tell Mr. Neville why his wife had summoned him up to the house. If he had, Neville would have cleaned up and made himself presentable for company. Instead, Neville barged into the living room in full farming regalia—dirty high top boots, an old hat rimmed with sweat, and shreds of fabric across his back and chest from what had once been a shirt. He wore long khaki pants decorated with patches of mud, some dried and caked, some still wet, all interspersed between grass stains and actual plants that clung to his pants. Neville came face to face with my father and the five of us. His embarrassment was almost palpable. For a brief moment, he seemed immobilized, trapped in a room from which he could not retreat. My father stood up and motioned for us to do the same. The threat of our approach galvanized Neville. He mumbled something inaudible and rushed around the edge of the room, through the dining room, and out of sight. As he passed inches from a large standing fan, the breeze offered us the aroma of pig. His wife explained somewhat awkwardly that he would be back when he got cleaned up. This did not take very long in real time, but the uncomfortable silence seemed to span hours. My siblings and I looked around the room and mostly at the front door as we stole sly glances at dad. None of us looked at each other. The embarrassment of the moment had enveloped us all. Neville's wife and dad tried to have some semblance of a conversation, but the lively vivaciousness of the earlier greeting outside was gone.

To stem some of the self-conscious discomfort of the initial entry, Neville re-entered the room with a tray on which were two shot glasses and a bottle about one-third full of rum. He approached, talking as if he had been in the conversation before and had merely been interrupted. This time when we were introduced to him, he smiled and shook hands. He commented on how tall the boys were and how one brother, Mark, looked exactly as my father had when he was younger. He said that I looked like one aunt and Lyn like another aunt. He and my dad each had a drink and Neville began, first haltingly and then with gusto, to regale us with some of the experiences that he and our dad had shared as boys and later as young men. While Neville was regaining control of the visit and himself, his wife furnished us with drinks and some sweet biscuits.

We had been there for about one half hour when we heard Neville's daughters approaching the house. They would have seen our car out front, in which case it would not be unusual to approach the house via the back door, so as not to intrude, if one's parents were entertaining. As soon as Neville heard the girls in the kitchen, he sent his wife to get them to come and meet us. The two girls entered the room with mincing steps and downcast eyes. Overweight, acned, black geishas in training, I thought wick-edly. They approached us with the deference of servants and ex-tended warm hands, limp as cooked noodles, for us to shake. As they went down the line with five hands to shake, one of them managed a reluctant smile while the other hurried through the process, averting her eyes from us and anxious for the ordeal to be over. Mission accomplished! Neville had met Fred's children, most of them anyway, and Fred's children had met Neville and his family, but it ended there. There would be no furtherance of this friendship into the next generation, I concluded in silence. After the girls had darted back into the kitchen, my father broke the ensuing silence by asking Neville about his hogs. Neville was com-fortable with this topic and very proud of the success he had been having breeding and selling hogs for decades. He went into some detail about his farming techniques and his business in general.

I don't know if it was in this conversation that my father's plan was hatched, or if it came later, but at some point that year, my father made an agreement with Neville to pay the full price for one of Neville's young pigs. Neville would continue to rear the pig to adulthood and at Christmas the pig would be slaughtered and evenly divided between both families. This plan reached my ears just before Christmas when my mother was explaining to a friend, through whom she normally placed her Christmas order, why she was not placing her usual order for pork that year. My mother did not seem enthused with the idea. She may have had misgivings about how well-cleaned the pork would be, as she did not know if there would be a trained person butchering this animal. This was not a grave concern however; it just meant that there would be more work for her in preparing this pork, if the preliminary stages had not been well done.

It was agreed that my father would go for the pork the day before Christmas Eve. As arranged, my father was up and out of the house just after breakfast, to get his half of the pig at Neville's. The pig was to be slaughtered that morning. If my dad had just driven there, picked up the pig, and driven back home, he would have been home by noon. It was expected that he would visit his mother and sisters so that arrangement would have him home by early afternoon instead. Mom had all the seasonings cut up and placed on the counter prepared to receive the pig.

Noon came and went, as did early, and then late afternoon, and early and late evening. It was the end of the day when we were ready for bed that we heard my dad's car pull up. Looking out the window I saw him go to the trunk of the car, reach in, and lift something with both arms outstretched. I knew it was his half of the pig. In my mind, the half pig was going to have his snout and feet, hair and hide, and I was curious to see it up close. I rushed to open the door as I saw dad turn toward the house and mount the step to the front door. He walked briskly toward the kitchen with his load and deposited it on the kitchen counter. I followed a few paces behind him. Mom was in the kitchen waiting. She too had heard the car pull up. As dad put the pork on the counter, he turned to mom, but before he could say anything, we were all fiercely assaulted by the stench of rotting pork. Dad seemed as surprised as we were. He approached the load on the counter and lowered his head to it and inhaled. I suppose he wanted to be sure of the source of that foul odor. He lifted his head from the pork and turned to face my mother. She had her arms tightly folded across her breast and took on the demeanor of an army sergeant as she said very slowly and very clearly, "Fred, please get that thing out of my kitchen." Dad did not utter a word. He just looked at the pig as it lay there in silent rebuke. Then obediently, and rather humbly, he retrieved the pig and retraced his steps out the front door. I don't know what he did with the pig, and I did not hang around for his return. I left my mother, talking to herself as she put away the seasonings and wiped the counter with a strong disinfectant, and sneaked quietly into my bed next to my sisters.

Christmas was a season of excesses. Drinking was done in excess; hanging out with friends was done in excess; and there were no age barriers in this regard. My father had picked up the pig early as expected. What was not expected was my father taking his best friend with him on the trip. The two had stopped along the way and visited other buddies, many of whom were also professionals in the field of education, and all free on vacation with nothing preventing them from having a good time. And so it was, that my father spent the day eating, drinking and laughing with his friends while the Christmas pig, snuggly encased in the hot car trunk, fermented under the blazing sun.

God's Child Prevails

I have already established that my mother considered herself to be God's child and we heard this often, as she highlighted all the little miracles that took place in her life on a regular basis. I was decades into my adult life before I fully understood what God's love really meant and developed an appreciation for every gift that God gives. Armed with this new insight, I was in awe of the frequency with which I could see Him deliver His blessings, now that I was looking closely. My mother lived her life in total appreciation of God's love. She, therefore, understood that as a child of God she had a duty to pass on that love. I put it in these words now, but my mother passed on God's love so effortlessly and with such sincerity and humility that one would never have considered her many acts of kindness to be a duty. It was just her nature and her desire to be kind and generous to all who came her way.

I remember Julia, an old lady who came to our house weekly for food until I left home. I don't know how my mom was first put in touch with this lady, but she came every Sunday at a time agreed upon. Usually, mom would have all the dishes ready and Julia would wait only long enough to get her containers filled and bagged with very tasty food to last her for a few days. On the few occasions when my parents had company or some other event that would delay mom's schedule, my mother would dart quickly around the small kitchen, her eyes constantly on the clock, because she did not want Julia to have to wait. She was more conscious and diligent about the meal being ready for Julia than she was for invited guests. Despite her efforts, there would be times that Julia would arrive and the meal would not be quite ready. On those occasions, mom would add a soft drink to the package and take it outside to Julia at the front gate so that she could apologize for keeping her waiting. On the days that Julia looked especially frail, mom would make one of my brothers walk home with her to carry the heavy food. Of course they never really walked with Julia. They always walked ahead of her, reaching her gate long before she did, then have to wait for her. There were a few weeks when Julia did not show up at all, and mom would have someone go to her home to see if she was alright and carry the food for her. This would take place before our family sat down to our Sunday lunch.

My mother knew of another family that was frequently in financial distress. Usually, on a Saturday, one of the older boys from that family would come to my mother with a note from his mother, Mary, requesting help. Often, my mother did not have any money of her own to lend, but she would keep the boy in the house playing with us long enough for her to get someone to lend her the money to meet the request. At those times, I always asked why she would take that risk of borrowing money for someone else when she did not have it herself. Then we would go through that routine where she would remind me again about casting bread upon the water and having it returned. Again, in my great wisdom, I would point out that wet bread is unpalatable, only to have her smile at my response. I would also give my view that if she did not have the money to lend, she had no further responsibility in the matter. She would explain that Mary had no one else to turn to in her time of need, but my family had more access to people who had an extra dollar or so to spare. Mom was always confident that Mary would repay the loan in a timely manner, and she always did.

Once, my mother found out that one of my brother's friends often brought just plain bread to school for his lunch. My brother did not carry any lunch himself, because school was close to home and he would go home for lunch. After my mother found out about his friend, every day she gave my brother a nice big sandwich and a drink to carry for him. On the few times when she did not have the sandwich ready, she made my brother bring the friend home with him for lunch. Our lunch meal was the main meal of the day, so it was never just a sandwich. I know the friend was happy for those days because my mother was, among other things, a great cook. We had daily religious education classes, retreats, regular mass, and everything else that went with a catholic education, but none of those nuns, priests or rituals taught us the true meaning of God's love and God's Word as our mother did in her daily activities.

My mother's numerous acts of charity and her catholic duties never caused her to neglect her other duties. She just moved faster. Mom could be seen running from the kitchen to the bedroom several times a day when she was making her nine-hour *novena,* or hurrying to mass before breakfast on weekdays when she was making her nine-day *novena.* And if that wasn't enough, she fasted every Friday, for an entire year, for no reason that we could fathom. It was a standing joke in our family that she was "more catholic than the pope." As we grew up, we began to be aware that we were beneficiaries of her great sacrifices; and, as we grew older yet, we began to rely on her—as if she were a magician—not just for ourselves, but for our children and even for our friends. If someone was looking for a job, having a difficult pregnancy, experiencing marital problems, facing financial challenges, or wanted to pass an exam for which he or she had not studied, we passed the requests on to mom. We fully expected that she would intercede on our behalf to God or St. Anthony, whom we referred to and whom she wisely acknowledged as "her Boy."

In the later years, when mom had no children living at home, her many acts of kindness would have rivaled, easily, the department of social services, if one had existed. She was *meals on wheels* and *elder care* all rolled into one. If we happened to visit mom and dad at lunchtime, dad would be at the table alone, waiting for mom to return from her rounds, so they could have lunch together. Dad delighted in updating us on the number of people she was helping to care for at any given time. Sometimes he would jokingly inform that today mom has another shift, as Mr. so and so needs a bath and his wife can't do it on her own anymore. Mom did not drive, so she did all of these errands and provided all these services on foot. Dad had long before ceased to drive, as glaucoma had claimed most of his sight. Dad enjoyed teasing his wife for her *Good Samaritan* qualities, but he actually supported her a great deal, and I am sure that he was very proud of her as well. He was well aware that he had been very blessed to have had her for a wife for over 55 years until he passed away in 1999 at the age of 87.

My mother told me, and her friends confirmed it, that her deep abiding faith in God began in her youth, long before thoughts about a husband and children were ever conceived. Marriage and motherhood offered more people for her to pray for, so her devotion became, if anything, stronger and more intense; so intense indeed, that even Satan found her too powerful to reckon with when he went after her in a powerful way.

It was 1952, and we were living in a deeply rural area in central Trinidad. My father had been assigned by the Catholic Board of Education to Coryal R.C. School as principal. In 1952, my father did not have much seniority as a principal, having only been confirmed in that position for four years. As a junior administrator, he received the least appealing assignments, which he had to accept (taking his family—then wife and four children—with him). Coryal, at that time, was an area without electricity and indoor plumbing in the homes. There was running water in government buildings and schools, but this water came from concrete cisterns where rain water was collected and filtered. It was then made available for bathing and other household purposes, but it was unsafe for consumption. Some homes had cisterns as well, but most had just large oil drums in which the rain water was collected and then taken into the home for use as needed. All water for drinking had to be boiled; water for bathing was warmed primarily by the sun; a bath at noon time or early afternoon was best. Water for an early morning bath or for a child was warmed on a coal stove, inside the house, and put in a bucket in the bathroom. Water was then dipped from the bucket for the bath. With my father as principal of the school, my parents enjoyed the economic position that allowed them to have domestic help. So, as primitive as life was, the actual hardship on my family was severely reduced by the fact that there were people to fetch water, clean, cook, and help with the children. My mother was able to assist where she was needed in the community and in church. She also spent a lot of what we would now call "quality time" with her family and, of course, she had lots of time for prayer.

My parents did not have a large group of friends in this area, so on weekends we often visited my grandmother and two spinster aunts in my father's home town of Sangre Grande. With so many children, there was always a lot of packing to do if we were to be away for an entire weekend. Three, of the four of us children, were little runners—old enough to make trips from the house to the car—packing toys, shoes, and pillows that went directly into the trunk and did not require being put in a suitcase (known, then to us British Colonials, as a *grip*).

On one such weekend, my mother arrived at my grandmother's to find that only one side of her house slippers had made the trip with us. The left side was nowhere to be found. It was assumed that one of the little runners had dropped it in the yard en route to the car, which was parked in the front of the house in the part of the big yard closest to the road. My mother borrowed a pair of slippers from my grandmother for the weekend, and no one thought much about the situation again, until we returned home and the slipper was nowhere to be found. It was not in the car, which had been emptied on our return; it was not in the yard, where we expected to find it; it was nowhere in the house, the closets, or under the bed. Mom had worn both slippers the day we left and now one of them had disappeared. This was strange, but not worrisome. It was just an inexpensive pair of slippers, which could easily be replaced, and was within a few days.

No one thought about the missing slipper again or even mentioned it. No one had any reason to think about it when my mother developed a dark blue dot on her left foot, just below her instep. No thought was given to it when the instep of that left foot began to swell, then hurt, or when the pain intensified so much that my mother became disabled, unable to walk. When the news of my mother's mysterious illness spread through the small village, many people dropped by to offer cake, ginger beer, very tasty meats of all varieties, but mostly they came with advice of all kinds. Those who lived in the immediate neighborhood came by every day at first; then, as time went by and there was no change to her condition, they just sent their regards, good wishes and occasionally some home-made fudge or coconut candy.

There was, however, one woman who never stopped coming. She was an old woman of African descent who was known for her practice of Shango—a religion that has its origins among the Yoruba people in Nigeria, Africa. In Trinidad, the term Shango refers to the entire religion while in Africa it is the name of one of several Yoruba gods. More significantly, the beliefs and rituals are closer in practice to Santeria in Cuba and Voodo in Haiti with some customs from Catholicism sprinkled in for good measure.

Despite the sweltering hot weather in Trinidad, this Shango-practicing woman always wore several layers of clothes. No parts of her legs were ever exposed, and she wore tall boots usually worn by men. No one ever saw her hair. Her head was always wrapped with several lengths of cloths in varying hues. She was very serious and inspired fear. Everyone called her "Ma Bay," and some adults and most children kept a safe distance from her on the street. She frequented our home to collect all of our empty bottles from cooking oil, vinegar, wine, rum, medicine, soft drinks and beer. There was no size or shape bottle that Ma Bay did not collect. Some she turned in to the local grocer for money, others she stuck in the ground upside down at measured intervals along the edge of her property. The effect was eerie—assorted glass, planted as if expected to sprout.

When Ma Bay came to see my mother, she was not content to just inquire about her. She would be quite insistent on actually seeing and speaking with my mother. Her questions seemed to be seeking a medical update, not just polite neighborly interest. The young women of the village, who helped with domestic chores, had a great dislike for Ma Bay and warned my mother not to have her come near her. My mother laughed at their fears and was her sweet kind self at all of the visits. There came a time, however, when my mother could no longer walk to the living room to see Ma Bay. Mom would not have her visit with her in her bedroom; instead, she would speak with Ma Bay through her bedroom window.

One day, Ma Bay asked to be allowed to hold one of her religious meetings in our front yard. Seeing no harm in it, my mother gave her permission to do so. The meeting began at dusk with a lively crowd. Some of the attendees were actually members of the religious group, while others were just curious onlookers. After more than two hours, Ma Bay, her group dwindling to single digits, was still preaching, shouting and jumping up and down with several large flambeaus dangerously near to the pillars of the house. My mother sent word discreetly to ask Ma Bay to bring the session to an end. It was bedtime and my father was losing his patience with the ruckus and had threatened to end it in an ungracious manner. On getting the request, the woman who only moments before had been claiming a divine connection, got into a grand rage, she spat ferociously on the walls of the house, kicked the open flames of her flambeau and stormed off the premises. The next day, however, she still came by for a complete medical update on the patient. Even when there was nothing new to tell, Ma Bay seemed to pry for information.

The colony at that time had a sparse selection of medical professionals, but they had been very well trained and some highly specialized. All were trained in various countries in Europe, mostly England. They were held in very high esteem and well respected. My mother availed herself of the expertise of some of the best doctors, each referring her to another and yet another. Though visiting the doctors from our remote location sometimes meant being away from home overnight, my parents spared no expense; pursued every lead and suggestion; and followed up on every referral. Each doctor seemed more mystified than the one before. There was no system or organ in the body that could be responsible for my mother's curious ailment. Her problem was extremely localized. Her only symptom was excruciating pain in her left foot and an equally tender place on the bottom of that foot marked by a large black dot, which seemed to get darker with time. The doctors did not think it was an infection, as there was no accompanying fever or inflammation; the discoloration had not spread, even after several weeks; there was no change in her appetite, behavior, or other functions, except her sleep, which was severely interrupted by the intense pain. Despite several tests and consultations, there was no official diagnosis.

The number of domestic workers in the house was increased for a short while, as now all of my mother's chores and responsibilities had to be taken care of by others. It became uncomfortable having so many non-family members in the small house, so one weekend my father went to visit his mother and sisters and returned with his mother and a large suitcase. She had come to take charge of the household.

Despite the fact that most nights my mother had very little sleep, and despite her intense and constant pain, she always put on a brave front—at least in front of us children. I don't know if mom had been expecting my grandmother, but when she saw her and her large suitcase that my father was carrying behind my grandmother, she broke down and sobbed. She embraced my grandmother who had tears in her eyes as well and they hugged for a long time.

For mom, my grandmother and her suitcase signaled that someone reliable was going to be in charge. That relief could have caused the tears. Grandma and the suitcase also implied that preparations had been made to replace her for quite a while, signaling a lack of faith in her recovery. That too would have been just cause for tears.

Grandma settled in and mom stayed in bed, now, all the time. At dinnertime mom would crawl to the dining table and by the time she got there she would be in tears because of the pain. Seeing her cry and seeing how tedious and painful it was for her to walk that short distance, caused me to cry too. Having my grandmother living with us was great for all the usual reasons. She also kept my mother laughing and distracted from the pain. My grandmother gave mom every herb and grass concoction she knew. She made poultices of every variety and put them on her foot. She anointed the foot with a variety of oils. My grandmother was of African descent, and had grown up in Venezuela until early adulthood. When she moved to Trinidad and married my grandfather, they lived in a rural area for decades. She was, therefore, versed in remedies indigenous to both countries and I think she tried them all, in an attempt to cure mom. After a while, the medical doctors merely renewed mom's prescriptions for codeine to deal with the pain and ceased to schedule further office visits. After all, there was nothing they had not done already, and they had no further insights into her case.

My grandmother had always cherished her daughter-in-law as if she had been her own daughter. My mother's own mother had died when my mom was just four years old. Her mother's best friend assumed responsibility for her and eventually became her stepmother, when she married my maternal grandfather. Both these parents had died the year my mother married my father. Her stepmother died just months before the wedding and her father just months after the wedding. My mother had no siblings and no really close relatives. She was glad to embrace my paternal grandmother and to return the love that was shown to her. During my mother's illness, my grandmother took good care of her. They also talked and laughed a lot. She regaled my mother with stories of my dad and his siblings and of her own experiences. Mom was still suffering a great deal, but having my grandmother there made everything easier.

One morning my mother described being awakened by a noise that sounded like giant birds flying around on the roof. She lay still for a while but could not identify the source of the very loud unusual noise. Despite how loud she thought it was, my father, a sound sleeper, lying next to her did not stir. After a while, curiosity got the better of her and, hobbling as best she could with the furniture for additional support, she got herself to the back door of the house and opened the upper half of the door.

Exterior doors were often made in two parts with each opening separately. The top half was often opened while the bottom part remained closed. Doing so allowed air to circulate through the house without the risk of small domestic or wild animals like the mongoose, which were known to inhabit the area, entering the house.

As the upper door swung open, a neighbor began shouting excitedly, "You missed it! Oh! You just missed it!" Then she explained with great animation and eyes popping, that she had come to her window to throw something out and had seen a huge bird, bigger than she had ever seen, on our roof top. She said it was so white that it seemed to exude light and it was just circling the roof of our house. She said that she had been so mesmerized by it that she was unable to call anyone from her household to see it. Interestingly, my mother was the only person in our household who had heard it. After exchanging the usual pleasantries with the neighbor, my mother pivoted on her right leg, prepared to slowly hobble back to her bed. Miraculously, she found that her pain was all gone and she could put some weight on her left leg. She returned easily to her bed and sat silently for a while. She knew she had been healed and she knew that somehow the white bird was a symbol of the miracle that she knew she had received. She began to weep and pray. Both startled my father out of his sleep. He leapt to the floor expecting that something bad had happened, but mom was smiling through the tears. Dad was so confused that it took him a while to register that she had gotten up and walked normally to the window and back twice. Then she sat again on the bed, extended her leg, and asked him to look at the sole of her foot. She knew what he would, or rather what he would not see. Her foot was smooth and soft to the touch and there was no black mark.

My father was particularly silent that day; in fact, so was everyone except my mother. She spent her day giving thanks, singing hymns, and occasionally weeping ever so softly. Before lunch was over, my grandmother and her *grip* were leaving the house washed thoroughly in the tears of the entire household, including my father and the women who were employed in the house.

This story would have ended there and the mysterious illness would have been buried, except that five years after this incident (four years after we had left the village and were living in the city of Port-of-Spain) the daughter of the neighbor who had seen the big bird came to visit. That family had remained living in Coryal, as it was their permanent home. However, because of the lack of opportunity there, the family members with the potential to benefit from secondary education, had come to Port-of-Spain to avail themselves of such, and went home to Coryal only on some weekends. One afternoon after school, this ex-neighbor, Lara, now in her late teens, came to spend some time with us. As a young child, she had been particularly fond of my mother, and my father had identified her potential when he taught her in school. So, she enjoyed visiting with us. She got to chatting with my mother, updating her on her family and the other people that my mother cared most about and of whom she had inquired. She informed my mother that Ma Bay had suffered a psychotic break. What she really said was that Ma Bay had gone mad. This was not much of a surprise, since Ma Bay had never seemed completely sane anyway. Lara said that Ma Bay had been boasting about her supernatural powers and all the ways in which she had used them. The part that Lara was anxious to relate was that Ma Bay was claiming to be responsible for my mother's illness. She told all who would listen, that she had found that slipper in the yard and used it to "fix" my mother. She said that my mother's faith was too strong, hence her recovery. She was not meant to recover from the "fix" or "hex." Those of us who heard this revelation were stunned into silence. My mother was unmoved by the story. She insisted that Ma Bay was trying to look important and was using her illness to promote herself. My mother refused to give evil any credibility or power.

   The loss of a cheap slipper was not something that would have been publicized in the village. This insignificant event, five years earlier, would not have been known to the reporter of this story. The fact that Ma Bay disclosed this so many years later, the mysteriousness of the illness, the relationship in time bewteen the disappearance of the slipper and onset of the illness, made this disclosure more than plausible to me. No one who knows the story can conjecture any possible reason why my mother would have been the target of anyone's wickedness. But, not knowing the reason does not mean it did not happen. Whenever this story is told, it has skeptics raising their eyebrows in polite disbelief and others sharing similar stories of their own. To me, it is a wonderful miracle story of God's love and commitment to us and of the unrelenting faith of my mother, "God's child."

Mayaro

hen I was growing up, if there were people who enjoyed exotic vacations in foreign lands I did not know them. Going to the seaside for a few weeks, was as exciting as vacations got. In the group comprising our friends, playmates, and neighbors, we were among the few privileged enough to go to the shore for at least two weeks every year, courtesy of my two spinster aunts, Mattie and Simona.

Each year my aunts rented the same house from a family friend. The house was in a seaside town called Mayaro, on the southeastern shore of the island. My aunts invited my two older siblings and me to stay for the entire two weeks, perhaps because we were closer in age to their two adopted daughters and required minimal supervision. I refer to Laura and Earline as adopted daughters, but they were never legally adopted and their status in the home was somewhat of a cross between an adopted child and a *restavec*—a term used in Haiti to refer to a child sent by their parents to work with more affluent family members. The child's role is akin to a domestic servant. In exchange the child receives food, shelter, and an education that the parents could not have provided otherwise. Laura and Earline's status leaned toward the adopted because though their chores seemed a lot, they never did the labor-intensive tasks like cooking or washing and ironing. They did do all the dishes, a lot of the cleaning, and prepared lighter meals like breakfast. They considered my aunts their mothers, loved them, and were loyal to them to their deaths. The fact that they inherited significant property from my aunts suggests that the feelings were mutual. To us they were cousins and very good friends, and we all looked forward to those two weeks together.

Sometimes two of our younger siblings went also, but only for a few days. More often than not, the four younger ones stayed at home with our parents and would visit the first weekend that we were there and then again for the last day or two of our stay. My aunts were both educators—Mattie, a school principal and Simona, an assistant school principal. On their vacation and during their leisure time, they did not want to be responsible for younger children who might have required more supervision or care than they felt competent or willing to give, in addition to the time they would have needed to give to their mother, our grandmother who came with them. Elbert, Lyn, and I were generally well-behaved and obedient—at least when we were not at home—so we were no problem to them. We added to our aunts' enjoyment or at least made them feel altruistic in providing their brother's children with a vacation that we may not have had otherwise. Now, I say this only in hindsight because they never made us feel like they were doing us a favor. We always felt most welcome and were quite pampered.

My aunts seemed to have an inexhaustible supply of candies, cookies and treats that we were offered all day. At home, when we came in from playing, we satisfied our thirst with water. In the house in Mayaro, there was always available a gigantic mug of the most delightful mix of fruit juices, with lemon always one of the flavors in those drinks. This made it most refreshing on a hot day. We were well supervised but did not feel restricted. When we wanted to go somewhere that my aunts might not have been very comfortable with, they would let us go, but would take the opportunity, themselves, to take a walk so they could keep an eye on us. They would be so far behind us that we were unaware of their presence. In this way we felt free, but they knew we were safe. In the evenings after dinner they participated in our storytelling and provided us with great insight into their life growing up with our dad. The stories were funny, and it was good to hear about dad's childhood from their point of view. The stories were consistent with those that dad had already shared with us, but we liked hearing them again. During game time (there was no television), if we were playing a board game, one aunt in particular would facilitate cheating by discreetly distracting an opponent who, until that moment, had been ahead in the game. There were other games in which they actively participated. They even taught us some new games that involved a lot of laughing. Whatever they got out of having us on their vacation, we had a great time and created wonderful memories with them.

The first year I recall going to Mayaro was 1959. I was 10 years old; my older siblings, Elbert and Lyn were 14 and 13 respectively; Laura and Earline were both 14. The tradition continued until 1963. In 1964 Mattie was preparing for retirement and there was quite a lot going on during that time (she was also relocating from the area in which she had been stationed for work), so the decision was taken to skip Mayaro that year. By the next year, 1965, Simona was dead. She was killed in a motor vehicle accident that April. I was 16, and my older siblings 19 and 20, had been outgrowing that kind of vacation since 1962 anyway, so we never vacationed in that house in Mayaro again.

During the five years that we vacationed in Mayaro there were many other families who owned or rented vacation homes every year at this same seaside resort, and soon we had a community and vacation friends. As the years went by, we added newcomers to our small group. Some people ceased to return for one reason or another and so the community lost members as well. It was constantly changing.

The Stewart family, a widow with three children—one girl and two boys—were among the families we got closest to. The older boy, Terry, was Elbert's age and he fit in well with us. The younger boy, Encose, was about eight years old, but was treated by the rest of the family as if he was a baby or handicapped. He was catered to in every way and even things that an eight-year-old was capable of doing, were done for him. Someone had to help him into and out of his swim trunks, and everything he ate or drank was brought to him. He never had to exert any energy in getting things himself. When we first met them, I looked closely to see if there was any sign of infirmity or retardation. I found none. As he was very quiet, I thought he was shy. I changed that opinion when I heard how loud and demanding he could be when his needs were not being met to his satisfaction. Every year as we anticipated meeting the family, I expected that he would have changed and become more sociable; he never did.

His mother developed a relationship with our aunts, and as the children would play on the beach on moonlit nights, the three of them would sit together and chat. Encose stayed with the grownups. My sister and I expressed our curiosity to his sister, Pam, hoping to get a story on him. She dismissed our inquiries and did not seem bothered by his demanding personality. She behaved as if it was her duty as his older sister to minister to him. She was only 12. The older brother seemed to ignore him as much as possible. I overheard my aunts talking one day and I got the impression that in some way, which was not clear to me, the family's attitude to Encose was related to his father's death. The father had died when Encose was six years old and there seemed to be a connection between Encose and his father's death. Since we could not get the true story and we knew that the father had died suddenly, and at home, we conjectured that Encose had discovered the dead body or in some way had been responsible for his father's death. We were just trying to make sense of the unusual dynamics in that family.

Dynamics notwithstanding, the Stewart family was the closest to us in the community. We found that we had a lot in common, in terms of what we did at our homes, the type of discipline instilled by our parents, and the hobbies we enjoyed. From the laughter that would come from the grown-up section, we knew that our aunts had also found a kindred spirit in Annette, the children's mother.

During the daytime, the adults were not together, but Terry and Pam did everything with us. Once they persuaded a fisherman to take us out in his boat for a little ride. We knew that we should not have gone on that adventure, but just before the boat was about to push off into the sea, I saw my aunt Simona in the distance with a hand in the air waving it from left to right. I chose to believe that she was waving us goodbye and thereby gave her consent to the trip. So, at the very last minute, the three of us jumped into the boat and joined the Stewarts. No sooner had the old fisherman left the shore with the five of us in the boat, than it began to rain heavily.

From the time the first drop of rain hit, I wanted to go back. I was surprised at how quickly after leaving the shore we were in very deep water. By this time the people on the beach could not be recognized except as moving specks. One speck kept moving rapidly in one direction and then the next. Pam began to cry and asked the fisherman to take us back. Now the rain was pouring; water was beginning to fill the boat; and the old man, who had appeared friendly and harmless on the shore, now seemed intent on scaring us as much as he could. He threw a small cup in our direction, instructed us to bail the water, and insisted that he was heading for the Atlantic. I had no sense of direction then, but I knew the Atlantic was a big ocean and I thought that we were going to die. Pam attempted to get up and move toward the edge of the boat, but this only made the boat unstable and made us all even more terrified. The fisherman now seemed menacing and began to taunt us with threats of leaving us in the ocean or taking us to another island. We all just sat still and all the girls cried softly.

We continued this way for what seemed to be a very long time; then the boat began to approach land again. We saw the shore coming to us and we dared to hope. We were careful not to say a word to the man we now thought was mad. When we were able to recognize the area, we knew that we were more than a half mile from where we began our journey. As soon as we were in shallow enough water, the boys lifted us and practically threw us out of the boat. We did not want to risk being taken back out to sea. Without a word to each other, we began to run as fast as we could in the shallow water toward the shore.

In the background we could hear the crazy boatman laughing and shouting, "Same time tomorrow?" Pam, who had such bravado at the beginning of the trip, was still sobbing and wiping her eyes with the back of her hand. She also seemed to be moving very slowly, and under different circumstances we might have found all this very funny. My feet grew wings and my sister kept my pace. My brother and Terry ran slowly so that we would stay ahead of them.

When we got to the spot where we had been picked up, we saw our aunt. She was drenched to the bone. Always poised and dignified, Aunt Simona now looked like a madwoman who had just been rescued from a shipwreck. As we approached, we could see that she was visibly relieved and very angry, and if we thought she represented solace, she did not. She stood still as we reached her and all she said was, "I will see you at home." I think she was too emotionally drained to say more than that.

When we arrived home, I was surprised to find that what seemed like an endless ordeal on the water had all taken place in less than 40 minutes, including the time it took us to run from the drop-off point to the house.

We were already dried and changed and had food placed in front of us, though none of us had any appetite, when my aunt arrived home. She went to her room, asked for coffee and asked to be left alone. We gave the story to Laura and Earline who had stayed at home to help with the mid-day meal. They told us, when they carried the coffee to my aunt she added brandy to it and she was smoking a cigarette. She had long before given up cigarettes, so we knew she was very upset and that we were in serious trouble.

When my Aunt Simona emerged from her room more than an hour later, she informed us very calmly that she was going to contact our parents and we would have to go home the next day. When I explained that I thought her hand signal meant that she was waving goodbye and it was okay to go into the boat, she almost exploded. She considered that anyone would know that her hand waving from left to right and right to left so frantically, was clearly saying "no" to what we were considering. Why, she asked, would she be waving goodbye to us so enthusiastically since we had just left home minutes before and were expected back by lunch time. She made sense then, but my interpretation had conveniently made sense to me at the time too. She never contacted our parents and we did not go home, but we never did anything remotely dangerous after that.

Vacationers to Mayaro were not all like the Stewarts. They came from different parts of the island and from all walks of life. The wealthy visited more than once a year and owned large homes in the area. They were known to us, and they were known to each other, but I daresay...we were not known to them. Another group who we referred to as "free spirits" were young people who seemed to have no connections to the area and were content to camp on the beach. They were generally friendly, and seemed to get along with the residents. It seemed we ran into them everywhere; in the shops, on the beach, and even in church. Yet others appeared to be on extended visits with grandparents or other family members who lived in the town, or were working professionals like my Aunts, on vacation in rented houses. It was from these latter groups that we formed more lasting relationships.

The house, in which we stayed, was situated on Radix beach. It was a solid brick house with three sparsely but adequately furnished bedrooms. Aunt Mattie and my grandmother shared the master bedroom, which had windows that provided an impressive view of the sea at high tide or low tide. The second bedroom was the exclusive domain of Aunt Simona, and the third bedroom was shared by all the girls. Lyn and I shared the only bed in the room and Laura and Earline slept on individual cots. My brother had no bedroom. He kept his clothes and other belongings in our room, but slept on a big sofa in the living room.

The living room in this house did not offer the formality or the order of those in city homes. It was the room in which we gathered after dinner for activities together, or where we did our individual reading when the weather outside was not inviting. Every member of the household was an avid reader. The room was bright and inviting and the floor was always gritty with sand because the front door was always wide open and only a small porch separated this room from the outdoors. From the living room or the porch, my grandmother, who was now not very active, would enjoy the ocean, the beach, and whatever activity she could see from the house.

The rest of us spent very little time inside. I was always an early riser, and in Mayaro, the sunrise was a great incentive to rising early. When I woke, the cousins would be awake—already preparing coffee for the adults—but otherwise, the house would be quiet. I would go outside and sit on a large log that leaned against a post in the front yard where the land sloped into the small incline that was the beach. I would sit there and enjoy the start of the day when the noise of the ocean was the only sound, and rather than disturb, it encouraged my thoughts. At these times, I did think about, or miss my parents and younger siblings, but that only lasted until breakfast. My longing for my family was more than amply soothed by the spectacular sunrise which waited for me beyond the horizon and came into view slowly enough to allow me to savor every color and every sparkle that bloomed into existence. And, if this picturesque event was not enough, I was at the same time gently fanned by the salty sea breeze that brought with it the cleanest scent on earth-truly fresh air. It was a remarkable way to begin the day. Into adulthood and to this day, whenever I experience a sunrise, sunset, or a particularly pleasing seaside environment, I remember that serene and beautiful time sitting in front of that house in those carefree days in Mayaro.

***

The different groups in Mayaro had their special activities; but, all the groups generally converged for one event that happened daily, the common purpose of "pulling sein." The vacationers young and old, small and big, and many of the villagers, would wait on the shore when they saw a fishing boat heading inland or heard the loud horn that was blown to announce the event. Once the boat came in, everyone would line up one behind the other, each holding on to the edge of the fishing net to help the fishermen position the fish into the center of the net and haul the catch unto the shore. This was more challenging than it sounds, and if there was a really big catch, the net would be very heavy indeed. When the fish were all brought in, those who helped bring in the catch could help themselves to the very small fish, which had little commercial value. We would string them through their gills on a strip of palm branch and proudly take them home to be fried to a crisp and eaten with hot hardough bread. Sometimes we got to pull sein more than once for the day; we really looked forward to this. Otherwise, we spent a lot of time frolicking in the sea never tiring of the breathtaking scenery and miles of shore that made Mayaro beach the longest and possibly most beautiful beach on the island.

The beach and its environs were unspoiled and represented, to some extent, the simplicity of life at that time. It is what one would conjure up if asked to envision a typical island beach. There were no man-made dressing rooms; there were no car parks;

no big commercial buildings. There was nothing to interfere with the elegant lines of palm trees bowing gracefully in the wind to the majestic ocean. No one cleaned up the many pieces of driftwood scattered along the shore nor the empty bottles or other knick knacks discarded by the ocean. To us, these were treasures around which we could create stories and which we often took home as mementoes.

On our strolls along the beach, we would run into people we knew from school and who were there only for the day. We chatted with villagers and bought food from vendors, just to get the opportunity to talk to them. One afternoon during our third vacation in Mayaro, we were walking on the beach when two handsome young men joined my sister, brother, two cousins, and me. One of the young men was clearly smitten with my cousin, Laura. He had been sneaking glances at her even before they had the courage to approach us. His friend was there for support. I was only 12, but all of the others were well into their teens. Laura, Earline and my brother were 16, my sister was 15 and their interest in the opposite sex was being awakened. The young men, who both looked to be about 18 or 19 years old, strolled with us and engaged in chit chat about mundane things. After we introduced ourselves to each other, we talked about our life outside of Mayaro. They were both from the south of the island, were close friends and were in Mayaro for the first time on vacation. They had made day trips before but had never stayed overnight. Now they were here for a week, and this was their third day. They were very evasive about where they were staying and we did not care enough to pursue the matter. Our interaction with them was so short-lived that I do not remember either of their names. As we strolled, the smitten one positioned himself next to Laura and made it clear that he wanted to talk to her exclusively. His friend spoke to my brother a lot, but included the rest of us as well.

I don't recall anything that transpired in our exchange, but not long into Laura's tête-à-tête with her admirer, the rest of us overheard a conversation from which it was clear that there would be no love connection. We knew immediately that Laura's suitor was not someone we could invite over to meet the adults at home. He was not even someone we could really engage in a friendship, for despite his impressive stature and good looks, his language was abysmal. It was difficult to listen to him and not give in to our childish and cruel inclination to laugh at him. He had grave difficulty mastering even the verb "to be." Since we came from a family in which teaching was the predominant profession and other members who were not teachers were senior civil servants, we might have been somewhat snobbish toward people whose grammar was inadequate. Speaking proper Standard English was always enforced in our home and the ability to do so was given great importance.

As we were all enjoying our stroll, and Laura the attention of this young man, we overheard him telling her about his job at one of the oil refineries in the south of the island. It was a mechanical/technical job and he was describing it to her in some detail so that she could understand. When he had finished with the details, he summed up his presentation proudly by saying, "Yes, so that's the work I does." Except for my brother, we excused ourselves and, we hope, escaped without being rude, as we ran into the water and dived in to let the water muffle the peals of laughter that ensued.

Two nights later, we were sitting on the beach in the moon-light playing games—some traditional and others we made up as we went along—to entertain ourselves. My sister suggested a game in which someone would present an acronym and the rest would guess what it stood for. The person who answered correctly would get points based on the number of attempts that was necessary to get to the correct answer. After a set number of incorrect answers, there would be no points to be given, and the person who gave the challenge would tell the correct answer and would receive a high number of points for having stumped the group. Each one of us tried our best, therefore, to come up with obscure or little known acronyms to present, in order to win points for the game.

It was Elbert's turn and he presented *TTWID*. It was unfamiliar to us so we guessed the best we could. We posed every combination of words that would fit, most beginning with "Trinidad & Tobago" as that seemed a reasonable option. Long after the points had been exhausted we continued to guess just to not be outwitted by my brother, who looked so smug and seemed confident that none of us would get the right answer. Finally we gave up, regretting that with the points from this answer, he would win the game. We were prepared to concede defeat, but none of us was prepared when he looked at my cousin Laura and said, "*TTWID* stands for That's The Work I Does." He burst out laughing and took off running dodging the large balls of moist sand flying in his direction.

***

The summer vacation months coincided with crab season. This was the season that crabs came out of their holes at night and recklessly roamed the beaches to be caught and relished by human predators. In the crab world, I am sure there was good reason for this roaming about, like perhaps releasing their eggs into the sea, but for the villagers it was time to go crab hunting and have barrels of crabs to sell to city folk like us.

The first year that we visited, the villagers shared with us the technique for catching the crabs. They carefully demonstrated, on already captive crabs, how one held both ends of the *boat*–a hollow husk that grows on coconut trees and holds its flowers when the tree sheds. Found in abundance beneath the coconut trees, which grew profusely along the beach, this naturally occurring tool is about three feet long, shaped like a canoe or boat, and smooth to the touch. It is also flexible but firm so that it can be bent in two to imprison the fleeing crab in the hollow cavity. The coconut boat was the only tool that was needed and the villagers gave that to us too. Prepared as we were, in theory, to hunt and catch crabs, and armed to the gills with our equipment, torches, and excitement, our success was not impressive. We saw many crabs, which saw and certainly heard us, too. However, they scampered away to safety long before we had any chance of capturing them. As we hunted, we talked and joked as we did whenever we were together. The villagers had equipped us, but had failed to explain that noise would hinder us from catching any crabs. There were always at least eight to ten of us hunters and our footsteps resounded on the dry sand. At the sight of a crab, even at a distance, we would scream, run, and create such a ruckus, while at the same time trying to bend the coconut boat into the attack position. Only a suicidal crab would have allowed itself to be caught by us. Even the old and infirmed crabs were easily able to reach the safety of a hole before we hunters were upon them. That first year, I recall that we caught only one crab and it was dead when we awoke the morning after his capture. It may have been ailing, which would explain why we were able to catch it in the first place. It's also possible that it died from the trauma associated with its capture.

The second year we thought we would be more successful. We limited our group to the five from our household plus Pam and Terry Stewart. Again, the crabs were abundant on the beach; we were quieter but, as each one of us tried to catch a different crab, we ended up bumping into each other. We ran like crazy people, literally in all directions, and the crabs scampered back into their holes. Elbert managed to snag one crab, but not with his coconut boat, which he found ineffective. He went for the crab with his hands. Well, that method was not in the instruction manual, so he was not prepared for the intense pain that seared through him when the crab held on to his finger. His screams brought us all running to him. He was making bad matters worse by trying to shake the crab lose from his finger. When Pam saw the situation she began shouting, "The eye! The eye!" This only caused us to direct our confused attention to her and to her eyes then to my brother's eyes, all the while he was still screaming in pain. We took our boats and began to beat the crab. This just caused the finger to tear more. The crab would not let go.

Meanwhile Pam was still shouting, now hysterically, "The eye! The eye!" Our commotion brought a young couple to our assistance. The man positioned Elbert so that the crab was on the ground and not dangling from his finger in mid-air, and within seconds he had released the finger from the crab's claws. It seems that if one holds down the eye of the crab, it opens its gundies. Pam knew this, and that was what she was trying so ineffectively to convey by her repetition of: *The eye! The eye!* We were not impressed with her explanation, which was too late. We went home immediately after the release to attend to my brother's wound and retired from the sport of crab hunting forever to the dismay of Mr. Tommy, a local who kept tabs on our futile nightly exploits.

In the mornings, after the days on which we would announce to all and sundry that we were going crab hunting, Mr. Tommy would delight in asking us how we did. We suspected that he knew even before he asked that we had had another unsuccessful night. Mr. Tommy may have been laughing at us behind our backs all the while. If he had, it would have been only fair, as Mr. Tommy provided no small measure of amusement to us as well.

Besides our core group comprising the five of us from our home and the two Stewarts, there were at least three other persons who were with us a lot of the time. There were twin boys with very unusually tiny heads. Each one answered to the name, Twinny, and we just called them the Twinnies. They were 13 when we met, and were in our group in the first two years of our being in Mayaro. There was also Jenna, a girl who had no siblings, and who was my age. She came in the first and third years and was part of the group in the daytime activities only. Her mother did not allow her to participate in the nighttime activities because she said there were too many boys in the group and she had no brother to ensure her safety. The nighttime activities, besides the crab hunting, consisted of telling scary stories and making up games. The younger ones played hide and seek, but even in year one, my brother and sister at 13 and 14 would not indulge in that. Just being out in the night was a treat in itself. The nights in Mayaro were remarkable. The moon and the enormous canopy of stars shone brighter there than any other place on the island.

We met Mr. Tommy the first year that we went to Mayaro. He was an older gentleman of the ethnic group we refer to in Trinidad as "Panol." The word, I would wager, is a derivation of Español. This group was Hispanic in phenotype to the extent that there is a phenotype for any ethnic group. They often spoke some form of patois and were closely associated with parang music, a popular folk music which originated in Trinidad and Tobago and performed around Christmas time.

Mr. Tommy had lived in the confines of Mayaro all of his life. His view of Port-of-Spain, puzzled together from pieces he got from visitors like us and from headlines in the local newspaper, led him to believe that the Wild West lay beyond the outskirts of Mayaro. Mr. Tommy would read about a shooting in Port-of-Spain—the only one in five years—and respond as if shootouts outside of bars were the norm. Mr. Tommy talked as if gunslingers strolled down the streets armed to the teeth with smoking guns hanging from their hips. Because we came from such a dangerous world, Mr. Tommy seemed to delight in talking to us and sharing his views. Often my older brother would deliberately feed Mr. Tommy's imagination by giving him little bits of information, like the story of a man running down another man with a broken bottle outside of a bar in St. James. This was designed to send poor Mr. Tommy gasping, making the sign of the cross, and thanking God that he was far from it all.

For all the years that we vacationed in Mayaro, spending time with Mr. Tommy was something that we always did. We got attached to him first for the rides he let us have on his donkey, and then we grew fond of him for himself. First we laughed at him, like when we had a very heavy-set friend, Barb, with us one year and Mr. Tommy, wishing to know her weight, and if she had ever weighed herself, asked, "You ever scale on a scale?" Another time he told us about his daughter, who had gone abroad and of whom he was very proud. On that day he expressed concern about her stability because, as he put it, "The guhl leave England and she gone London." In later years though, we laughed with him. We really looked forward to seeing him every year even when he no longer had the donkey and we no longer cared to ride it. Mr. Tommy's house was a small brick house situated on a very large piece of land, just about a mile from the central village of Mayaro. Apart from the donkey, Mr. Tommy had other large animals and many chickens; some were in pens and some roamed freely. By 1963, Mr. Tommy was a friend whose company we truly enjoyed. Many years after we had ceased to vacation in Mayaro and even as adults, my siblings and I would wonder out loud about Mr. Tommy and though he must be long deceased, we still remember him fondly when we recall some of the most delightful memories of our younger years.

Plate Licker

During the 1950s children led active lives and engaged in physical activities at school and in their neighborhoods. Island life was not conducive to kids being overweight and only a few extremely privileged and over indulged children were fat in their teen years. Video games had not been invented and though television was part of life in America and Europe, it had not yet taken hold in Trinidad. Staying indoors only exposed children to additional chores, since adults always needed help. As a result of all these factors, young people practically lived outdoors.

One afternoon, about ten of us were just drifting without purpose and kicking sand as we strolled along the beach in Mayaro when we got to a large house—one of the nicer properties in the area. We had seen this house many times before in our walks, but it seemed to be mostly unoccupied.

On this particular day there were two girls, in their early teens, on the porch. Both were in swimsuits and completely engrossed in the meal before them. The older girl was very overweight.

Her face was round with no discernible chin to lengthen her un-usually short neck. Her arms, torso, and legs were also round.

The girls were so focused on their plates that they paid no at-tention to our approach. As we were almost abreast of them, the older one, having eaten every scrap of food off her plate, held the plate firmly with both hands and ran the full length of her tongue from bottom to top of the plate. She made several tongue strokes and then rotated the plate and repeated this action. Those of my group who first saw this, nudged the others and we all stopped and gazed at the fat girl licking the empty plate. When she became aware of our rapt attention, she blushed fiercely and stumbled over her chair as she darted inside the house and out of our sight. We were hysterical with laughter at the entire scene and at that moment she became, and was forever after, "Plate Licker." For the rest of that vacation whenever we would see Plate Licker, we would put open palms close to our face and mimic the action of her licking her plate. I think this action and our sheer numbers made her afraid of us and she would run when she saw us approaching.

Back in Belmont where we lived, there was a private girls' school next to our house. We were not old enough to know or care about accreditation of the school, but we held the view that the pupils there were girls whose parents had more dollars than sense. The school, we thought, offered a kind of remedial educa-tion for the upper middle class. This school was very small and was housed in a part of a large house that was occupied by two widowed sisters. The entire school population was contained in the living room, dining room and porch of the house—most in fact, being on the large open porch. One side of the porch was open to a main, heavily trafficked street and I wonder now how students could have studied with so much distraction as came from that street.

The students of this school stayed always in the confines of the school building or more correctly, the house. They ventured past the gate, which opened directly onto the sidewalk, only to be picked up by parents or by a driver. That school dismissed well after the catholic school that we attended, so often we got home before all the girls from the school had been picked up.

It was early in the school term, a few weeks after our return from Mayaro, when, as I was entering my gate, I heard laughter coming from the sidewalk of the school next door. I turned my head in the direction of the laughter and found myself looking into the surprised, incredulous face of *Plate Licker*. She may have been at that school for years, or she may have been new. I don't know if I had ever seen her before. If I had, I had no reason to remember her; but now that she was *Plate Licker* from our vacation in Mayaro, I would recognize her face anywhere. I think she was just as surprised as I was for us to run into each other on our home turf. I was so surprised that I did not have the presence of mind to mimic the plate licking action. Truthfully, without my siblings and friends with me for support I don't think I would have done it anyway. Besides, the openness of the seaside gave some privacy and anonymity that the main thoroughfare of Belmont Circular Road did not. I would have drawn unwelcome attention to myself, had I performed the action on the sidewalk. By the time I got my siblings to come out to see *Plate Licker*, she had either been picked up or was hiding inside the school.

During the months that followed, we caught many brief glimpses of *Plate Licker* but she avoided us as much as we avoided her. We ceased teasing her in any way, though we did make jokes with each other about her when she was out of earshot.

One day I was just getting home when I saw my uncle leave our yard and walk toward a car that had just pulled up in front of the school next door. The driver got out of the car and greeted my uncle very warmly in the street. As they were exchanging pleasantries, I saw, to my surprise, *Plate Licker* come out of the school, put her book bag in the car, walk around the car, and kiss my uncle. The three of them stood together for a while, then father and daughter got into the car and my uncle walked back toward our home as the car drove off. I had made sure that I could not be seen while observing the exchanges.

When my uncle came back into the house I was able to *pick* information about *Plate Licker*. I found out that *Plate Licker*'s name was Jill, her father was Frank. They had been neighbors and close friends of my uncle and his family for many years. Three years earlier, when Jill was 12 and her sister 10, their mother had died suddenly. The family was devastated by the death. They moved away, and since then their father, Frank, had been struggling valiantly as a single parent to raise his two daughters.

This knowledge made us all feel very repentant for having teased Jill so mercilessly those weeks in Mayaro. Having had both parents, especially a mother who was arguably the best in the world, our hearts really went out to Jill for having lost her mother at such a young age. Thereafter, whenever I saw Jill, I tried to make eye contact and I always smiled. Jill did not have any reason to change her view of us, so she continued to avoid eye contact, but she did not scurry. I know she was no longer afraid of any of us. I was happy about that. Instead of jokes or comments about her eating, we talked about how difficult it must be for her and her sister. We now felt protective of Jill and her sister and wished we could have started over and befriended them instead. The relationship never went beyond minimal eye contact and smiles from one side-ours. What we found out about her changed everything about how we viewed her, except that we could never think of her as Jill. To us then, and for all the years after, she remained *Plate Licker*.

The Cheese

Even if my father had never officially announced that my mother was in charge of matters in the home, it was evident that this was so. "Wait till your father comes home" was not a phrase with which we were familiar. Matters of chores, and most things that related to the children—their behavior, their activities, discipline, punishments and rewards—all belonged to my mother. Now having responsibility for dealing with something, does not always imply competence in dealing with same. There were many occasions when I believed my father would overhear a matter in session or maybe my mother deliberately carried a difficult case within his earshot hoping for his intervention. Whatever the impetus, my father would often get involved in matters being processed by my mother. At these times the case always took a more serious tone in the offender's view and resolution was speedy.

When we grew up, we marveled at the way in which my father was always able to get the reactions that he did from us. We would respond immediately to any and all of my father's orders.

We would do immediately on his command, things that my mother had been asking us to do all day or even all week. Or we would stop doing instantly, something that my mother had been asking us to stop for a long time.

My mother's method for administering medicine to us is an apt example. Mom would coax, cajole, reason, or bribe the person for 15 minutes and the recalcitrant patient would refuse to open his or her mouth to drink the ghastly medicine. My father would pass by a room and remark casually to the patient on his way to the bathroom "Don't let me pass back and find you have not taken that medicine." Those would become magic words. In fact any words from my father, especially those that began, "Don't let me find . . ." had the same effect. Long before he came out of the bathroom that medicine would be merely an unpleasant odor and taste in the individual's mouth. None of us ever found out what the consequence would have been if he had found us still with the medicine. No one ever let him find what he said he did not want to find. We would admit to my father things that we had denied to my mother and amend reports we had presented on fights, quarrels, broken items, etc. The truth would just roll out of our mouths almost before we had time to think. I say we marveled at his ability to change our behavior because, except for what my brother experienced, in his role as student, at school with my father, no one had ever been punished by my father. There was nothing in our experience that gave us any clue as to what the consequence would have been, had we not responded promptly to his directives. As an adult now, I suspect that my father himself would have been at a loss for a consequence had it ever become necessary. The anticipation of an unknown consequence was sufficient to keep us in line.

On one particularly memorable occasion, one of my siblings, fearing that he did not have enough time to cut a slice cheese, bit into the block of cheese and hurriedly returned it to the refrigerator before anyone could catch him. My mother was beside herself with disgust when she came upon the cheese sitting exposed on a shelf in the refrigerator. It was beyond her comprehension that her civilized children, with whom she had always worked at instilling good graces as part of ladylike and gentlemanly behavior, could be guilty of such a crude act.

She questioned us all, beginning with the usual suspects and going all the way to the ones she thought were least likely to perform such an act. Not surprisingly, every one of the six older ones denied culpability. My youngest brother was too small to be a suspect in the matter. My mother was truly angry. After exhausting all her techniques for arriving at the truth, she expressed her disdain at our disgraceful behavior and emphasized how disappointed she was in whoever had done the deed.

She was angry, frustrated, and helpless—helpless, until my dad passed by and inquired what was going on. My mother laid out the situation to him. My father took the offending piece of cheese lying on the kitchen counter and called us together again. With cheese in hand he asked no one any questions. In keeping with his usual record, he probably would have had a ready confession, but he was going for a confession *and* a dramatic finish. He asked each person to grin in such a way as to expose top and bottom front teeth. He looked at the teeth of the person in front of him and then at the cheese, then that person was dismissed, and the next person would present himself and his grin and the process would continue. Before we had all presented our teeth to him he found his mark. "Ahha!!" he exclaimed. "This is your man."

The person before him at that time was apprehensive and appeared ready to cry. He rolled his eyes toward the ceiling and tentatively bared his teeth in a tight grimace. My father had calculated correctly. The teeth patterns of the person in front of him matched exactly the teeth marks on the cheese. A confession would have been superfluous. He had identified the culprit through bite marks without the benefit of the high-tech forensics popularized on television shows like CSI. Back then, Perry Mason was our role model in these matters, and like Perry Mason, once he delivered the guilty party, he exited. Punishment was my mother's domain. This matter was either so out of her realm of experience, or so distasteful, that, except for repeating—this time directly to the guilty party—how she felt about his behavior, no further action was taken on the matter. The rest of us could not stop laughing, although we were careful not to be seen doing so by either parent or by the guilty party. We were sure the atmosphere surrounding that offense did not lend itself to public expressions of humor.

Family Values

When my parents bought the house in St. James, it had been large. As soon as we moved in, or perhaps before we moved in, my mother decided that we would use only four bedrooms and the fifth, the one nearest the kitchen, would be set aside for family meals, homework and other family activities. Although we ate more than we studied in that room, we called it "the study." The term family room or den had not yet been popular and none of those terms would have suited that room anyway. Study was the only proper term for a fifth bedroom converted to a place to eat and study, and remains so to this day.

Four bedrooms were quite sufficient for my family of seven children and two adults. My parents had the master bedroom and the three girls slept in an adjoining bedroom. The three younger boys were grouped in the third bedroom and the one, apart from the rest and on the other side of the house, was occupied by my oldest brother. Today, that plan would be called a split plan; back then, it had no fancy name. It just allowed my older brother more privacy than we thought he deserved.

I say my brother occupied the room, and not that it was his room, because of a point of view my father had espoused only once with lasting effect. He believed that a room cannot belong to anyone unless the house belongs to that person or that person is paying for the use of the room. This was not the case with us, so all the rooms belonged to my father and mother. None of the rooms belonged to us—a brutal concept perhaps for today's modern psychology, but in those days it kept things in clear perspective. This attitude enabled my father to establish an order that allowed us to co-exist happily within our limited means, and I believe it even helped to foster the keen sense of family that always existed in our home. Even so, we think that sometimes dad took this too far. The principle may have been sound, but sometimes the execution seemed harsh.

I recall one incident in which my younger brother Alan was required to wear "dress uniform" to his school on the first day of the new term. This consisted of a white long-sleeved shirt and dark blue, long pants, which we called: *dress pants*. It was September; the beginning of the school year, and unfortunately my mother had only just become aware of how much my brother had grown during the vacation. The pants that he had used the term before were way too short and too tight for him to wear. In the normal course of things, my mother would have taken that problem to my father for discussion and a solution. On the morning of the first day of school, my mother instructed Allan that he was going to use my older brother's blue pants for his "dress uniform" day. Elbert attended a different school and did not require dress pants at the start of school. When Allan went to get the pants in question, Elbert objected vehemently and went to my mother for an explanation. My mother told him that she had indeed instructed Allan to use his pants and if he wanted an explanation he should get it from my father. One wonders why he was naïve enough to make such an attempt, but he did.

Elbert approached dad for the explanation, while dad was shaving in front of the mirror over the sink in his bedroom. He told dad that Allan had been told to use his pants and he wanted to know why this was so. He explained to us later that dad continued shaving and, without even a glance in his direction asked, "Which pants are you talking about?" to which Elbert replied, "My blue pants. My new blue pants."

Dad feigning ignorance and focusing only on the foam on his chin, asked for further clarification. "Which blue pants are you talking about?" Taking the question literally, Elbert explained, "The blue pants that Papits made for me two weeks ago." Papits was the tailor.

Directing his attention now to the even strokes of his razor, along his jaw line and beneath his chin, dad replied, "Oh that pants. You had me confused when you said *your pants*. You see, I buy all the pants in this house," he continued, moving closer to the mirror to examine the spot he had just shaved, "therefore all the pants belong to me." Dad paused and rinsed the razor to underscore the insignificance of the conversation in which he was engaged, then continued, "Whoever I say wears those pants, wears them. Today Allan wears those blue pants." He proceeded to rinse the traces of soap from his face—a signal that the shave was over and so was the discussion. My brother left the room without another word. Allan wore his pants that day, and that was that.

I have seen the size of tables that are designed to seat eight persons; ours was not such a table, yet it seated nine. The entire family of seven children and both parents always sat together in the small study every night at dinner and for all meals on weekends. The study had a small sink and an oblong table with a custom built bench on one side, and regular chairs around the rest of the table. The bench allowed for more of us to be seated than chairs would have. My father sat at the head of the table and my mother, when she sat, was at his immediate right. I say, when she sat, because she was the last always to come to the table, and seemed constantly to have to run back to the kitchen for one thing or another. I don't recall that the rest of the family had specifically assigned seats, but we must have had specific seats if only out of habit. I only remember sitting across from my mother, but I cannot recall where anyone else sat, just that they were all there.

Despite the fact that as we grew up the older ones became involved in activities outside the home, it was always expected that every effort would be made to be home every night for dinner at seven o'clock. Apart from the fact that being at dinner was expected of us, a person missing the family dinner could easily find that on his arrival home there would be only, what could rightly be termed, trace elements of whatever we had had that night. My mother did not always remember to put aside the absent person's portions in advance of the meal being served, and it would have been asking too much to have sufficient left over for that person after the rest of us had eaten.

During the week, my mother had breakfast alone after we were all gone off to school and my father to work. Most of us carried our lunch and ate at school, because school was too far away for all but two of us to return home for lunch. When my brothers were in school with my father, they came home with him for lunch and my mother joined them. But dinner time and weekends were always family time.

I never needed any psychologist, sociologist or any other professional to convince me that meal time is a very important time for forming and observing a family. At our table, we talked freely and easily about our day. My oldest brother would regale us with tales about the boys at Fatima, the high school he attended, and about "Far Pantin" and "Far Laifook" (the teenagers' version of Father Pantin and Father Laifook). We would talk about the escapades of our friends and some of the injustices that teachers perpetrated on students at school.

My older brother undoubtedly had the funniest tales ever and he always had new ones. There was no real competition. In later years we suspected that his stories were so interesting because he had no problem embellishing them as necessary. He also repeated certain parts of the story for effect. My father did not often participate actively in dinner-time conversation and we had the impression that he made a special effort not to laugh at our humor. I suppose this was part of his theory that one should not be friends with one's children. My mother respected no such rule and laughed heartily, her ample bosoms bouncing up and down as she did so. Sometimes, when the humor was too much for my father to keep up the façade of not being amused, he would turn to my mother and pretend that he was laughing at the fact that she was laughing, and not at the joke itself. At other times we would see him visibly trying to refrain from laughing. His nose would quiver and he would "purse" his lips, but often the smile broke through anyway. It was enough for us to know that we amused him. If he chose not to laugh that was okay too.

Our parents would have had no excuse for not knowing what their children were about and what was happening in their lives. We were adult and employed before we reached the stage when my mother would ask, "How was your day?" and get the single answer: "Fine!" or ask, "What happened at work today?" and get the response: "Nothing!" As children and teens, we were nothing if not garrulous. We never deliberately told our secrets or those of our friends, nor did we narrate any accounts of punitive actions taken by our teachers against us, but unknowingly we gave enough information for our parents to have a pretty good idea of what was happening in our lives, in school, and among our friends. If we had a basement no one would have been able to build a bomb without being found out. No one would have been able to harbor or sell drugs, build an arsenal or execute any of the horrific news-worthy activities that we hear so often happening in homes today. I remember one particular situation in which this kind of dinner table chatter and routine accounting of daily activities solved a problem that had not even been recognized as being in need of resolution.

One day I had an altercation with one of the *sisters* at the school that I attended and she asked to see a parent. At the time I was surprised because the matter did not seem to warrant such a severe response. Prior to the week of the incident, sometime in the mid-1960s, the nuns had all been referred to as "Mother," and the priests were referred to as "Father." There was Mother Margaret Mary, Mother Theresa, Mother Angela, and many others. Following a decision during the period of *Vatican II*, a major event in the Catholic Church, it was decreed that the nuns would no longer be referred to as "Mother" but would have the title of "Sister."

In the Catholic school, appropriately referred to as the convent, which I attended, any occasion to be jocular or frivolous was coveted. On the first day after the ruling, the girls displayed more respectful behavior than they ever had before, taking every opportunity to say and stress the word "sister" as in "Good morning *Sister*," and "Thank you *Sister*." Toward the end of the day, this particular nun, whose entrance had been eagerly awaited, entered the classroom. The class gave her the loud and enthusiastic greeting, "Good afternoon *Sister*." She had either had too much of that for one day or was in a foul mood for other reasons. Her response to the class was abrupt and unfriendly. Perhaps feeling embarrassed for the class or just irritated with her, I responded to the rebuke of our good humor with a loud *steups*. More correctly I sucked my teeth. I thought I had done so discreetly for only my classmates nearby to hear. Well, Sister's foul mood may have sharpened her hearing or maybe I discharged more air than I intended. The result was that my *steups* was heard by sister who looked in my direction, pointed at me, and demanded that I leave the room until the end of the lesson.

I fully expected to be asked to account for my behavior. I planned to put forward that my *steups* was in response to my own irritation at being unable to locate a pen that I had earlier, and to apologize for sucking my teeth and that would be the end of that. Well I was wrong. I was never given the opportunity to give that excuse or any other for that matter. Instead I was told to have a parent visit Sister. I considered it much ado about nothing, but delivered the message to my parents. Of course, in presenting the Sister's request, I outlined the circumstances leading to her request and neatly appended my explanation as part of the incident. This was believed to be a minor incident and so my mother presented for the conference. I was not too concerned because I believed that I could not be proven to have done wrong. In fact I imagined myself unfairly treated if only because I was never asked to explain my behavior. The Sister in question was a very short, vain person who in the past had shown herself to be some-what arrogant and lacking in humility, like when she miss-spelled a word on the board and pretended she had done it on purpose to see if we were paying attention. Anyway, I considered that the facts were clear and there was no serious trouble ahead for me; of this I was convinced.

When I got home on the afternoon of my mother's visit to the school, I was dismayed to find my mother very serious. This was unusual for her. She was normally very welcoming when we got home and inquiring of our day. That day, after accepting my greeting, she told me that from what she had been told at the conference that day, she was very disappointed in me and that the visit to the school had embarrassed her. This was a shock. I expected she would be told that I talked too much—every teacher, since I was five years old, had that complaint. I expected that she would be told that I caused the class to laugh at my whispered witticisms, but to be disappointed in me and embarrassed was exceedingly confusing to me. Moreover, my mother would not tell me what exactly the sister had said. She apparently had to share this with my father first.

As soon as my father arrived home and greeted my mother, they went to their bedroom and closed the door. I was cold and very silent for the duration of their conference of which, try as I might, I was unable to hear a single word. I could not begin to guess what my mother could have been told by the sister because, except for my unsuppressed wit and frequent chatting, there was nothing negative that I could think of that would have been revealed to put my mother in such a mood. My academic performance was reasonably good and my parents were aware of those details. Quite some time had elapsed before my mother exited the bedroom alone. She appeared in no better a frame of mind and gave the impression of not being on good terms with my dad. There was an air of disharmony between them. Now I was really confused.

At dinner that night, my mother remained in a bad mood but now the displeasure was directed at my father, not at me. My father on the other hand, was quite at ease, not unhappy or displeased, and clearly had no issue with me. I was relieved but could not leave the matter alone.

The next day when my mother appeared to be her old self again, warm and caring, I ventured to ask her about her visit to my school. She was reluctant to respond, and only half-heartedly told me that the sister had reported that I was rude and insolent. My mother demonstrated this "attitude" with body movements that I concluded was conveyed by sister. She reported further that despite this blatant and almost vulgar response to authority, I never asked any questions in class when I did not understand any aspect of the lesson. There may have been more, but my mother stopped at this point and I dared not ask her more. I was speech-less. Who was this uncouth child that the sister had described? Why would a nun, a person of God tell such a blatant lie against a student? It took a few minutes to catch my breath and absorb this information. Too drained and disillusioned to put up a defense, I weakly denied the allegations. My mother asked, "So are you say-ing that the nun lied on you?" To her surprise, I said boldly, "Yes she did."

I was angry with my mother for believing what she had been told about me, and hurt that she felt I had disappointed her. She did not expect a nun to lie, but she would expect me to lie. She still believed all nuns were wholesome beings with only the best interests of their students at heart. At some level I was able to excuse my mother. Sister, however, I could not excuse. I wanted to go to her and shout in her face, "You liar! God is watching you!" And just in case God was not watching, I wanted to personally step on her habit and throw her off the platform but only after I had dragged her veil off and exposed her head, which until then I had been led to believe was as bald as an egg. I was disappointed in her and disillusioned that someone whose job it was to lead others in the right direction would lie so boldly on a defenseless student.

Many months, passed after this incident and I had put the matter out of my mind. We were at the dinner table one night and I was talking about two girls in my class who were generally just enough like me that the teachers often got us confused. I was relating how that day sister (the one who lied on me) was angry with Ann, one of the girls in question. Sister stood before the girl, stared directly into her eyes and said, "Marie get out of my class this instant." In my seat in the class, I was not in her range of vision nor had I done anything wrong. Surprised, I stood up and exclaimed, "Me Sister!!" At this point she turned to me confused and asked, "Who is Marie?" and then to the other girl, "Child what is your name?"

To me this was merely a story of mistaken identity that I was relating. Unknown to me, it was a triumphant validation for my father and a mortifying defeat for my mother. When my story was over, my father said pointedly yet in a semi-jocular manner, "So this nun does not even know you?" I was glad I did not get his meaning and naively explained that many teachers made that same mistake. I went on further to explain, in her defense, that this nun only taught us religion and so had us less frequently than teachers in other subject areas and knew us even less than most. At this my father made an indefinable grunt and assumed a broad smile, or perhaps it was a sneer, directed at my mother who pointedly refused to look in his direction. No explanation was ever given to me, and it was years before I was able to make sense of the exchange.

On the day of the conference, when my mother reported what the nun had told her about me—my parents always referred to the sisters as the nun, no names were necessary—my father had challenged the accusation. He considered, and rightly so, that he had a good idea of what each of his children was likely to do, and this charge did not fit at all with what he knew about me and my proclivities. My response to the allegations had been irrelevant to him. He had trusted his own judgment, and so had never said anything to me on the matter. My mother, a very devout Catholic, had never experienced anything negative from the church and her mind could not conceive of a person of God telling a deliberate lie without cause. She was prepared to set aside her knowledge of me in favor of Sister's allegations. She had been torn for a while, but her fidelity to, and complete trust in the church won. My mistaken identity story, especially coming as it did without an agenda and so long after the incident, underscored the fact that information given about a student could not be relied upon when the reporter proved unable to recognize that student in her usual setting. My mother never apologized or acknowledged any change of opinion on that particular issue, but in later years, she had to openly and very regrettably amend, to a significant degree, the high regard she held for the sisters. Her faith was not affected, but she became aware that even people of the cloth are first just people.

My father practiced his catholic religion just enough so that he did not set a bad example for his children, but he was not in awe of, nor did he have exalted views or expectations of people of the cloth. Sometimes I think my father had a lesser view of them than he did of *regular* people.

Men of the Cloth

*A*s a principal of a Catholic elementary school, my father had intimate dealings with the priests and administrators of the church. Their condescending, often arrogant, attitude suggested that because they were white and working in a predominantly black country, they considered themselves superior to the populace—regarding them as ignorant natives. Their attitude was unacceptable to my father and lessened his respect for them.

The priest managers were employees of the Catholic Board of Education, which was under the auspices of the Catholic Church. Their main responsibility was the religious welfare of the church community. In addition, they had general administrative oversight for the Catholic schools in their district. In the eyes of the community, and even the teachers, a priest manager ranked higher than the school principal. This power came from his role as a priest and not from any rank in the hierarchy of the professional educators. In actuality an individual priest had no power to hire, fire, discipline, reprimand teachers or the principal, or regulate school hours. He could, however, make recommendations to the Catholic Board, where his judgments would have some weight. Often, despite the fact that they may have had little or no experience in this area, these managers presumed authority that they did not have and succeeded in influencing school policies in their respective districts.

Not surprisingly, during the course of his career, my father had several altercations with the priest managers of the schools to which he had been assigned. On one occasion he related, he was assigned to a school in the seaside district of Cumana. The priest manager, an Irish expatriate who exhibited little respect for the culture of the people and the customs of the villagers, decided that the district school would not be closed on Monday and Tuesday of carnival as was the custom.

Carnival is an important aspect of life in Trinidad & Tobago. It was brought to the island by the French colonists, sometime between 1776 and 1789, but has since become an essential way of expressing individualism and creativity. It is a rich, cultural tradition that is deemed an annual celebration of life and a symbol of unity in the sister islands of Trinidad and Tobago. Considered by some to be the "world's greatest show," carnival combines the components of calypso, steel band, and masquerade (playing mas) into a harmonious pageantry of beauty and carefree abandon enjoyed by every sector of the population. The highlight of this festival takes place over a five day period and ends on the day preceding Ash Wednesday, which marks the beginning of Lent. On the Monday and Tuesday before Ash Wednesday, there is what is referred to as the parade of the bands. Throughout the island thousands of masqueraders parade in the streets in elaborate costumes, dancing to the loud and infectious music of the calypsos of the season. It is a magnificent spectacle in which most of the nation participates. These two days had not been officially sanctioned as public holidays, but there is very little work performed, although essential business places like banks, government offices, and many retail businesses remain open to the public. All schools had been given those days off for all of living memory.

The priest manager in Cumana, at the time, had different ideas. Not only did he inform my father, the principal, of his decision to have school opened on carnival days, but at mass on the Sunday before carnival, he informed the congregation of his views and his ruling with a warning that any breach would be reported to the Catholic Board. My father had tried to reason with the priest and explain the importance of this festival, not only to the young teachers, but to the parents and students themselves. The priest was unyielding. My father informed his staff of the decision, his views on the matter, and the efforts he had made to have the decision changed.

In those days, corporal punishment was the norm in schools. Teachers were allowed...no...expected to administer corporal punishment to children for breaches of discipline, as well as for unsatisfactory academic performance. On carnival Monday, children turned out for school in response to the priest's mandate, because priests were held in very high esteem and their word was respected as law.

The mood in the school was not good that day. Children were sluggish and distracted. They had never before attended school on carnival Monday. They had looked forward to carnival and all the enjoyment that came with it, and now they were in school. Teachers were angry. They had made plans with friends to participate in the events. To their knowledge, their school was the only one on the island that was in session and neither teachers nor students wanted to be where they found themselves that day. I will not speculate as to whether the discipline in the school was worse that morning or whether the teachers were taking out their frustrations on the students, but my father reports that corporal punishment was being administered for every infraction in every classroom, to the extent that he had to speak to individual teachers about what he was witnessing.

Whether or not the teachers anticipated the result of their action, or they did more than just administer reasonable punishment to the children that morning, when the bell rang for school to resume that afternoon, there were insufficient students present to warrant having classes. The school was officially closed for carnival by the principal; and the teachers, parents and students were able to participate in the most important cultural activity in the country. Neither the priest nor my father discussed the matter. In future years, there was no objection by that priest or subsequent priest managers to closing the school for carnival or the other recognized holidays, religious or cultural.

On another occasion, a priest manager who had been repeatedly frustrating my father in the execution of his duties, and who in my father's view had now overstepped the bounds of his managerial position and in so doing had disrespected my father, was pulled back into his place by my father who, in his anger, referred to the priest as a "dunce little Irish boy." Such insubordination, when reported, did not go unnoticed by the Catholic Board. These and other infractions were duly noted in my father's file and he was informed of them. As far as the duties and responsibilities of his job were concerned, my father was outstanding. Parents and teachers, as well as administrators were well pleased with his performance in every school to which he was assigned. He developed a reputation for excellence and was frequently deployed to under-performing schools to resolve issues. His personal lack of adulation for the Catholic authority figures remained an issue, however. My father continued to act on his principles and demanded the respect that he deserved, unmoved by the actions taken with regard to his career.

After several applications for a promotion to a senior administrative position, which was then called "Inspector of Schools," my father was reliably informed, by a priest who had been a close friend of the family, that a decision had been made in official quarters to deny him the position that all agreed he deserved. My father seemed amused by this information, ceased to apply for positions, and seemed to make an even greater resolve to challenge the system. I guess he figured he had nothing to lose.

Once, when *subs* was due—a fee that was paid every month by students in the catholic school I attended—my father asked, through me, to be told what that money was being used for. Surprised by the question, my teacher took it to the principal who told me to tell my father it was for toilet tissue and soap for the students. My father returned a message, by me, saying that he refused to pay the fee but would be willing to donate toilet tissue and soap. My dad was aware that these items were already being provided to the school by a government subsidy. The principal, a nun, sent a message by me, to say that she was disappointed in my father. She had known of him in the course of their respective careers but had not had any personal experience with him. My father returned a message that he was disappointed in her too. I recall when he gave me that message for her, he had a broad smile on his face. The next day, I suppose after he felt he had made his point, he gave me the money that had been requested in the first place. These incidents did not add to his popularity, but popularity in that particular group clearly was not important to him.

He was just a few years away from his retirement age of 60, when he was sent a letter inviting him to apply for the position that he had been so long denied. Having held him in exile for many years, the Catholic Board or Education had decided that it was time to bring him home. They may have decided that he had learned his lesson. He had certainly mellowed with age, and he did deserve the advantage of a more attractive retirement income which the promotion would have given him. True to his personality and consistent with his past behavior, my father refused to be brought out of exile at their choosing and on their schedule. He very graciously thanked the authorities for their gesture and for considering him for the position, but he declined their invitation to apply. My mother, a practical person, considering the income situation, wanted him to accept the position. My father, a confident, principled, and yes...maybe arrogant person, took pleasure—I am sure—in his response.

I was in my late teens when this happened. One afternoon, I overheard my father relating the circumstances to his friends. I recall the sense of victory with which he conveyed his refusal of the position. I remember being overwhelmed with pride, respect, and great admiration for him at that moment. I think I understood then, the mythical story of Sisyphus as I saw it played out in my own home. Like Sisyphus, my father had upset the gods and had to be punished; and, like Sisyphus, he prevailed over his punishment and was superior to his fate. Instead of being a proletarian of the gods and powerless, he was rebellious, and what was to constitute his punishment crowned his victory. He too could hold his head up high and conclude that "all is well" the gods had lost. He had won.

A Haunting That Backfired

If a house could have feelings and express an opinion, I know that the house in St. James was very pleased with the joyful presence, gleeful chatter, lightheartedness, and warmth with which we infused it. The circumstances surrounding the house had not always been happy. The departing family had sold the house in much haste after a grave personal tragedy.

The story told is that a teenage boy in the Moriah family had been in love with a beautiful girl who lived in his neighborhood and attended a prestigious school in Port-of-Spain. An older teen, who lived in the area, was in love with her too. One afternoon, this other young man saw the Moriah youth escorting the girl to her home. After she was safely inside, young Moriah was returning alone on his bike when he was accosted by the older boy. A quarrel ensued and young Moriah was stabbed savagely by the older boy. Young Moriah managed to drag himself home, holding his gaping wound, and collapsed on the porch. He was rushed to the hospital where he died later that evening. He was 17 years old. The traumatic event and the pain of the loss caused his mother to become severely depressed. In an attempt to save his wife, and protect the family from the memories of that tragic day, her husband put the house up for sale, intending to start over in a new location.

We got the story from neighbors but cannot vouch for the details or even its authenticity. Prior to our buying the house we did not know of the family's loss, but they seemed very warm and pleasant and I gather that the sale and purchase of the house had gone smoothly. I recall hearing my mother lament about Mrs. Moriah's loss and I know she prayed for the family. If she knew the details surrounding the death, she did not share it with us children, neither did we dare ask. When I heard the story, I remember feeling a great sadness for the family.

My older brother Elbert was, and still is for that matter, a person who could create mischief in almost any circumstances. He too heard the story surrounding the death and he convinced me and my younger siblings that the name of the girl, for the love of whom the murder had been committed, was engraved somewhere in the house. He did not say how the name got to be written in the house but he alluded to a supernatural phenomenon. For months after moving into the house, I would not allow myself to be alone in any of the bedrooms and anytime a mark or smudge was observed on a wall, I would examine it closely.

One day my brother informed us that he had indeed seen the name written as he had been told it was. He said that he would not show it to us because he did not want us to be afraid. Of course this had the effect of making us very curious and even more afraid, as he intended. After days of staying together and being afraid of darkness or quiet, we persuaded him to show us the name.

Not surprisingly, the name was in his room on the back of the bedroom door. Though we could not recognize what he had scribbled, just between the two hooks at the top right hand corner of the door, we accepted that it was indeed "Molly," the name of the girl loved by the two boys. This worked so well for our tormentor that sometime after this he came up with another death-related, supernatural feature designed to have the same impact on us. By then however, we had become involved with our new playmates in the neighborhood and his tactics were ineffective. He had lost his power over us and had not succeeded in really frightening us to any great degree. Even when we were sure that the story had been concocted by my brother to scare us, we were not too upset with him. We certainly never considered getting back at him until one day an opportunity that was too great to pass up, presented itself.

I had a friend called Janine, whose mother had met my mother when they both took a course in Chinese cooking at the local YWCA. One day Roslyn, Janine's mother, was going to care for an aunt who was very ill and close to death. Preferring that Janine not be around to witness that suffering, Roslyn asked my mother to allow Janine to spend the night at our home. Janine and I were elated. When her mom brought her over, it was quite late and the entire household except my mother and me had already gone to bed. Elbert was at the movies and Lyn was on a school trip. When Roslyn's car pulled up, my younger sister, Lul, woke up and she and I were the welcoming team for Janine. My younger sister fell asleep as soon as she got back into bed, but Janine and I had so much to talk about that we could not sleep. My mother kept shouting from her room, "Girls, go to sleep." We would get quiet for a while then pipe up again. Just before midnight, we heard Elbert come in and go directly to his room on the other side of the house. It was at that moment that I hatched a plan—one that would beat my brother at his own game of house haunting.

I knew that Elbert fell asleep very easily and would be in a deep slumber as soon as his head hit the pillow. Janine and I waited just long enough to be sure that he was asleep. Then, I went to his side of the house and called his name in a normal voice. He did not answer, so I knew it was time to put our plan into action. By this time, we had been quiet for a long enough time that both of my parents were asleep, which we confirmed by the different rhythms of their snores.

We left our giggles in our bedroom and with stone faces, approached my brother's room. The first part of the plan was to pull the jalousies open. Jalousies are louvered openings that date back to the 16th century and were popular in the Caribbean while I was growing up. Generally they are located on external walls. In this case they found themselves inside the house between my brother's bedroom and the dining room. This and other evidence suggested that this room had been added after the house had been completed. The jalousies were made of wood. When closed, the horizontal slats lie flat against each other like window blinds; in the open position, they are stacked parallel to each other and allow lots of air to pass between them. Some jalousies operate with cranks that close them, but these were held closed with a metal pin that was placed in a small hole found under the slats. We knew that the sharp noise of the jalousies opening was sure to wake my brother and so it did. Startled, he asked, "Who's there?" Janine pushed open the door of his room slowly and stuck her head in just enough for him to see the outline of her face and her long braids hanging over her shoulders. She replied, in her normal voice, "It's Molly." After my job of releasing the jalousie, I had stepped away from Janine's path so that we could sneak back to my bedroom where we recovered our giggles and buried them in our pillows. Before our hasty retreat, we heard the noise of a body part hitting against the iron bed-head and another against the giant oak wardrobe. We also heard an item, perhaps the alarm clock, hit the floor. As we hit our bed, the light from Elbert's room crept through the lattice work and we knew he was fully awake. He kept that light on the rest of the night and there is a good chance that he did not go back to sleep for the rest of the night.

Janine's mother was a very punctual person. She had said she would pick Janine up at six o'clock in the morning. At three minutes before six, Janine and I said our goodbyes and she went to the porch to wait for her mom so that she would not have to ring the doorbell or honk her horn and awaken anyone. Later, when I saw my mom taking my dad's coffee to him in the bedroom, I knew it was okay to go in and say good morning to my parents—something that had once been a family routine but had died a natural death. My older sister still honored it most of the time; my younger sister sometimes; I, usually when I wanted an opportunity to ask for something as I did now, with both parents present. I prefaced my request with the confirmation that Janine's mom had picked her up and that *she* had asked me to tell mom thanks for having her spend the night. I was deliberately vague about whether "she" was meant to refer to Janine or to her mother. Before leaving the room I asked my mom if she could keep secret, from all my brothers, the fact that we had had a guest the night before. She looked puzzled by the request and asked why I wanted that. I said it was a game we were playing and gave no further explanation. My mother would never lie, not even as a joke. Had I told her the full story, she would not have agreed to keep secret what Janine and I had done to my brother. She would consider it wrong. However, there was no moral issue in asking her to not mention a fact that no one was likely to inquire about.

All of the next day, my brother looked as if he was afraid. He did not leave the house all day, and he was not as talkative as he usually was. Many times I saw him pin and unpin the jalousie that had opened the night before. He put the pin in as lightly as he could and then he tried to make it open. The pin always held fast. I watched as he let the jalousie open several times then innocently asked what he was doing. He explained that the jalousie had opened the night before and he could not understand how it had happened. His tone was flippant, but I knew better. "Maybe it was a *jumbie*," I remarked casually, using the Trinidadian term for ghost. "Don't say that," he barked, still testing the jalousie to see if it could open on its own. I knew he was scared and I enjoyed watching him suffer. Janine was shorter than any of us girls. None of us had thick long braids. My brother did not know Janine by sight, he did not know her voice and he certainly did not know that she had been spending the night. He had no answers to what he had experienced the night before.

The following night, Elbert asked two of my younger brothers to sleep in his room on the floor. He said it would give them a feel for what it was like to go camping. They readily agreed but he was unable to persuade them that leaving the light on would simulate the effect of the moon. They insisted on the room being dark and they prevailed.

On Sunday night, the virtual campers refused to spend another night on the floor. Instead my older brother, at the last minute, decided that he wanted to try sleeping on the floor in the younger boys' room.

Monday evening when he came home from school, he set about forcefully sanding out Molly's name at the back of his bedroom door. He used his own money to purchase a small can of paint and not only sanded, but repainted the entire door. He never found out the trick that had been played on him. I, on the other hand, was smug and delighted with my success. I had beaten him at his own game.

Adrianna's Family

When I left Ma Lopice in Belmont, I could not have known that I would meet her counterpart in St. James. Her name was Adrianna and she did not live across the street, she lived right next door. Like Ma Lopice, Adrianna had a husband, Andrew Sr., and two grandchildren, Andrew Jr. and Ana. The grandchildren's story was a very sad one, at least to me. I was 14 when their tales began. At that time Andrew was two years old and Ana was only 10 months, and they were happy children.

Sometime in 1962, Adrianna had to leave her home for an extended period. She went away to a sanatorium to be treated for tuberculosis. TB, as it was more commonly known, was the cancer of the 1950s and 1960s. Many people died of TB and everyone was afraid of contracting it. Like AIDS today, people were embarrassed to be struck down by it and tried to keep it secret. They were, however, required by law to be isolated from the population and were treated at one central hospital outside of the city. It was following this event that Joan, Adrianna's daughter with whom she did not have a particularly good relationship, her husband, Ken, and their two small children, came to reside in Adrianna's home. The household was now made up of Adrianna's elderly husband (Andrew Sr.), Joan, and her family.

Andrew Sr. seemed to have a good relationship with Joan, his adopted daughter, but one that seemed unfairly weighted to Joan's advantage. Andrew Sr. did all of the shopping for food and toiletries for the family, then he hurried home to prepare the meals. He did all the cleaning and was responsible for all the bills. Once during the week, and every Sunday afternoon, he drove to the sanatorium to visit his wife. I don't recall Joan ever going with him.

Joan appeared to be a rather pampered young woman in her early twenties. She was slim and seemed tall to me, although she may have been about 5ft. 5ins. She had a pretty face with delicate features and short curly hair that was a light brown color, which I believed to be natural. Despite her soft, whiny voice, Joan had a very friendly and light-hearted personality and related to us like a big sister. I spent a lot of time with her as I enjoyed talking to her and helping with the children. Often she would fix my hair in grown-up styles and let me try on her makeup.

Her husband, Ken, was 12 years her senior and a very serious man. He worked during the day and was rarely seen out of the house in the evenings. Ken was medium height and stocky with a round face and big cheeks. He wore glasses occasionally, which hid his most attractive feature—his light grey eyes. I did not care much for Ken because, not only was he serious and unfriendly, but when he was at home Joan seemed distant from us and some-what tense. I believe he loved her very much, but I also believe he exercised undue control over her and that she felt obligated to do what he decided should be done, even if she disagreed. Sometimes I would catch her crying. I did not think she was really happy with him, so it was a great delight to us all when, one day, she informed us that Ken was going to England. The plan was for him to get a job and an apartment and send for Joan and the children later. When Ken left, I spent even more time next door with

Joan and the children. Now Joan was always happy and since she and the children would soon be gone, or so I thought, I wanted to make the most of the time I had left with them.

Ken arrived in England in early spring of 1963, after a long sea voyage. An entire summer went by before he got a job that paid well enough for him to afford a suitable apartment. I was happy for that. He wrote to Joan often and apprised her of his progress. She reported it all to me. In hindsight, she shared a lot with me considering that I was barely 14 and she was a grown woman with children. This was probably due to her loneliness as I don't recall her having friends or going out much when Ken was there or even after he was gone.

One day in late August, Joan called me over to her house and she was very excited. She had news to share with me. She read part of a letter she had received from Ken stating that he had found a good job and an apartment and would be sending three tickets for her and the two children soon. They were to prepare to leave at short notice. Joan seemed happy at the prospect of joining her husband in England and so despite my own feelings of sadness at their impending departure, I was happy for her.

Less than two weeks after the arrival of that letter, Ken wrote again. This time, the news was not as thrilling. He informed Joan that the apartment he had leased did not allow children and that she should leave the children behind and join him in England because he needed her. He promised in the letter that they would send for the children as soon as possible.

I was surprised and disappointed when Joan began making arrangements to comply with Ken's instructions. I was sure that she would not be able to bring herself to leave two-year-old Andrew and 10-month-old Ana behind, especially since she had no close relatives to take care of them. With Adrianna in the sanatorium, my family was the closest thing she had to a family of her own and my mother had not offered to keep the children. Joan tried to win my mother's sympathy for her dilemma, but it was hard to see her situation as critical. Because of the kind of mother that my mother was to her brood, she felt sure that Joan would stay with her children until Ken found a more suitable apartment for the entire family. We were all wrong.

Ken sent one ticket and Joan's search for a caretaker for her children grew frantic. Just days prior to her scheduled departure Joan told us that she had arranged with a retired nurse, who lived a few houses away, to keep the children until she sent for them. To my knowledge, neither Joan nor the children had any prior relationship with this woman with whom the children would soon be living. This did not seem like a good plan and I hoped that Joan would see that. I was wrong about that too. Joan stopped looking for a caretaker for the children and they spent more time with my family while Joan made the arrangements necessary for her departure.

The last days before Joan was due to leave, my family and I mourned her departure. I was sad that Joan was leaving, but that loss was overshadowed by the misery I felt for the two small children being left alone with a stranger, while their mother went off to be with their father because he said he needed her. Certainly the children needed her more. Could she not see that? My family pampered and indulged those two children more than ever before, but all of my interactions with them were eclipsed by a cloud of sadness as I anticipated what life would be like for them when Joan was gone. The children seemed to sense the impending doom. Two days before Joan's departure, Andrew and Ana grew very irritable and seemed to cry all the time. They were mostly at home now with their mother and I hardly went over to visit. I did not want to intrude on the little time that Joan had left with them, but mostly I stayed away because I was just too sad to be around the three of them.

Joan's departure was scheduled for a Saturday evening, and as was the standard in those days, she was going on an ocean liner. Air travel to England was considered a luxury and was very expensive for the average person. By the time Saturday came, I had not seen Joan for a few days and when, on the morning of her departure she came over to spend some time with my family, I thought she looked old and drawn and not very attractive. She also seemed very uncomfortable, especially in my mother's presence. She fidgeted a lot and she repeatedly said, perhaps to assuage her guilt as much as for any other reason, how sorry she was to leave the children. She added that she would ensure that it would not be long before they were all together again.

My family, except for my father who seemed not to share our feelings and who kept his distance from Joan in every way, was very sad all that day, but all prepared to go to the harbor to see her off that evening. She asked that I keep the children that night and on Sunday take them up the street to their new home. I readily agreed. I was eager to do anything to ease the children's pain. That evening when she brought the children over with all of their belongings, Andrew was inconsolable. Maybe because my entire family was crying, and his mother was crying too, or because even at the age of two he understood what was happening, Andrew cried for hours. I thought his were the saddest tears I had ever seen a two-year-old shed. Ana was quieter than usual but otherwise she was playful and curious as any 10-month-old.

When Joan was ready to leave, she came over to our house one last time and kissed the children. Andrew had not stopped crying since she had brought him over earlier. Neither he nor Ana made any attempt to go with their mother as she retreated to the vehicle in which her father was waiting to take her to the ship. Instead, Andrew pressed his head against my legs, held on to me and whimpered softly. When she reached the gate, Joan turned around and waved, no one responded. My mother and my siblings went down to the harbor to see Joan off. When they returned after midnight, the children and I were asleep. It would be hours before the boat would actually set sail, but the time had come for the non-travelers to disembark.

I thought we would all be in bed for the night, but instead I heard my parents talking. I could not hear all that my father was saying but I could hear my mother repeating, "No, Fred" and

"I don't know, Fred." I heard activity, someone moving around in the next room, and then my mother appeared at my bedroom door in street clothes. She informed me that she and I were taking Andrew and Ana up the street to their new home that night, not the next day as scheduled. This alarmed me and I began to protest. My mother did not falter or hesitate. She said clearly that my father was not comfortable letting the boat sail with the children in our charge because we had only Joan's word about the arrangements for their care. My mother had not spoken to their custodian, Ms. Mathew, and my father feared that when we went the next day to take the children, we might find that indeed there were no arrangements. My father had no faith in Joan. He seemed to have little regard for someone who would leave small children with a total stranger to follow a man, albeit her husband.

The sleeping children were carried to Ms. Mathew that night and she put them to bed. I was glad they had not awoken during the exchange because I don't know that I could have given these distraught children to a total stranger if they had been awake.

The next day, after a very poor night's sleep, I was anxious to see the children but I waited until my mother and I were on our way home from evening mass to visit Ms. Mathew. I had expected to find the children clean and well-dressed as they always were. Instead, Ana had on a soiled undershirt, her face was dirty and her hair had not been combed all day. She greeted us as she always did and seemed happy to see us. Ignoring her dirty condition, I picked Ana up, held her close against my fresh Sunday clothes, and smothered her with kisses. Andrew was in no cleaner condition, but he did not greet us at all. He stood against a far wall and could not be encouraged to come to my mother or me. I tried my best to contain the tears that welled up in me and I knew my mother was doing the same. My mother asked Ms. Mathew how the children had spent the day and she told us how stubborn Andrew had been. She said that she had withheld lunch from him that day because he refused to say, "Thanks." She had presented it to him again hours later with the same result; and at the time of our visit that evening, he still had not eaten because as yet, he had not said, "Thanks."

I wanted to grab that hungry little boy and run home with him. I silently cursed his mother and father for abandoning him. I also blamed his grandmother for being sick. I felt a good share of guilt myself, though I could not determine why. I felt responsible, just witnessing the event. I was very angry and could not look at Ms. Mathew for fear that I would say something totally inappropriate. I had to be careful also, because I did not want her to bar me from visiting the children. My mother gently commiserated with Ms. Mathew about how children can have a mind of their own and be so determined when they want to be. She also reminded Ms. Mathew that with the loss of his mother, Andrew was likely to be a little difficult for a while and might need some reassurance and love. Ms. Mathew held fast to her ideas. My mother suggested as sweetly as she could that perhaps Andrew should be given his meals and that treats could be withheld as punishment instead. Ms. Mathew did not shift her position. No change came from Andrew either; he would not even look at us from his forlorn location against the far wall. Ana remained snuggled quietly in my arms. Even as we were leaving, Andrew would not look up at us. He had been silent all the while, though he was quite a talkative child. When I approached him to say goodbye, he shrank back against the wall. I kissed Ana and put her back on the floor. My mother put her arms around me and we both cried silent tears as we walked home.

Our family prayers were answered and the children's time at Ms. Mathew was short. Their grandmother, Adrianna, was well enough to be sent home from the sanatorium and immediately took the children to live with her. At this time, everyone expected that the children would be joining their parents before the end of the year. My relationship with the children remained close but not as close as before. Grandmother Adrianna was a very difficult person. She was always reluctant to have me take the children out of her house and the intense supervision and complaining at her home made my time with the children unpleasant. To her credit, Adrianna always had the children nicely dressed and very well fed. Treats were abundant and she invited other children over to play with them. As before, their grandfather, Andrew Sr., did every chore around the house including most of the childcare. He was also the only wage earner. His salary was modest and despite great promises, Joan and Ken did not send money to help support the children now that they were with their grandparents.

A few months after they were in the care of their grandparents, Joan wrote saying that they were anxious to have the children with them and that they would be sending for them as soon as the lease on the apartment was up. She did not say when this would be, and no one would have guessed that it would be as long as it turned out to be. The lease expired in due course and then the weather was too cold for the children. Since they were not used to cold weather, arrangements were to be made to for them to travel in the spring. When spring arrived, there was a shortage of funds for the tickets because Ken had changed jobs and was going back to school. The promises of reunification came often, but they were always followed by the excuses. The time was never right.

Weeks turned into months and the months became years. The letters to the grandparents dwindled to a couple times per year. The grandparents were getting older and were financially strapped. With two young children added to his responsibilities, poor Andrew Sr. did not have a minute to himself. The chores were endless and they were all his. He may only have been in his mid-sixties, but the rimmed glasses and carelessly dyed hair made him look much older and gaunt. He gave the appearance of being very frail but indeed he was not. Soon the children began school and they needed clothes and books and school supplies. Their grandfather worked even harder and never complained. Adrianna continued to dress the children like royalty and to have lavish birthday parties for each one every year. She also complained and said horrible things about Ken and Joan to the children and anyone who would listen.

Andrew and Ana's life with their grandparents was not bad, but it could have been a lot better. Watching the relationship develop between Ana and her grandmother gave some insight into why Joan and her mother had such a poor relationship.

Ana was a pleasant child and made friends easily. She lived only a few doors down from the elementary school that she attended and her little classmates liked to follow her home. At first she would invite them in and bring out her toys to play. This was alright as long as the other girls handled the toys well and did not demand more than Adrianna considered reasonable. At the slightest hint of discord among the children, Adrianna would loudly and viciously remind a child that the toys did not belong to her. It was not beneath her to tell the child that her parents were too poor to afford the toys they had the privilege of playing with at her home. She was known to actually snatch a toy out of a child's hand and give it back to Ana. These outbursts hurt and upset Ana and she would do all that she could to calm her granny and protect her young friends, but she was no match for the viper personality of her grandmother.

As Ana grew up, the friends she brought home were older. Sometimes they were the same childhood friends who had gone with her to secondary school, sometimes they were new friends that she had made in her new school. Adrianna's meanness took on a different tenor. Now she made indecent remarks of a sexual nature about the girls whose young bodies were taking on their distinct female characteristics. She would imply from their size the most unsavory things about their characters. She made remarks that were totally unfounded and very disturbing to all within earshot. She would, for no apparent reason, repeatedly tell Ana that her friends were insincere and were merely using her. Ana was neither rich nor famous, she was not from a privileged group and had no special advantages anywhere, and Adrianna was never able to explain why her friends were allegedly using her. She just used these remarks to undermine and erode Ana's confidence and self-esteem and a good job she did at that.

When Ana reached the appropriate age she began to become interested in boys. Though plump, Ana was not an unattractive girl and she maintained that pleasant smiling personality from her infant years. She had bright, animated eyes and a lovely head of thick dark hair. It was easy for boys to be interested in her and many came home to visit. When this happened, Adrianna seemed to lose her senses completely and describe in graphic detail the sexual favors she thought the boys wanted from Ana. She would say these things to Ana within earshot of the boys or she would shout them from her bedroom for all to hear. Ana often attracted very nice, well-mannered boys from good families, but one exposure to Adrianna's crudeness and vulgarity was sufficient for most of them to lose all interest in her. If Ana expected a boy to visit her on a Saturday afternoon, she would plead with her grandmother to try to be nice to him. She would tell her grandmother every good thing she could think of about the boy including in one instance that he was an altar server and very involved in his church. This did not have the effect that Ana had expected. Instead of making the boy acceptable to Adrianna, it gave her reason to speculate loudly (when the boy was visiting) about the relationship he might have had with the priest. He not only lost interest in Ana as a girlfriend, he never spoke to her again.

Not surprisingly, as Ana grew older she stopped inviting boys to visit her at home. Instead she met them away from home and went out on dates. When she returned home however, Adrianna was always waiting. Ana would try to rush through the gate as soon as she alighted from her date's car and would be met by a barrage of abuse. If the boy had already driven off or walked off she would ignore the abuse, but often the more chivalrous of her dates would insist on seeing her inside and they too would be assaulted by Adrianna. A few guys believed they could tame the beast and continued to see Ana. One relationship lasted almost a year until they broke up as a couple, for reasons of their own. This young man was tall and robust and very handsome. When he did not run away after Adrianna's first onslaught, he changed the dynamics between them. When he came to visit, he would greet Adrianna with confidence and look her in the eye. He did not attempt to make unnecessary conversation, but he did not shy away from her either. In fact she began to retreat when he was around. Others had treated Adrianna like a crazy person and either ignored what she said or answered her appropriately and continued to see Ana. As time went on, however, Ana as well as her beaus became frustrated by the situation. Dating Ana entailed too much stress. Ana had fewer and fewer dates and in the end she never married.

Andrew Jr. was a quiet child. Even as a very young boy, he did not engage in much play with others. He did very well, academically, throughout his school career but he did not have many friends and kept to himself. He was not encouraged to participate in sports or other activities and in his teens had a few select friends but was not known to date. He had an immense talent for the arts and excelled in this area as an adult. He was not comfortable with girls although he was always very close to his sister.

As the children grew up, not surprisingly, they began to take on Adrianna's abusive characteristics. While Joan had been affectionate with her father and gentle in making her demands, her mother was crude, loud, and brutal. The entire neighborhood could hear her shout, "Andrew, the rice burning." I often wondered why she couldn't turn the stove off herself. "Andrew, rain coming; pick up the clothes on the line." Maybe the blue dye in her hair would wash away if it got wet in the rain? "Andrew, yuh wet the plants? Andrew, yuh feed the dog? Andrew, somebody at the gate!" There was never an end to the orders, questions, and criticisms hurled at that old man. From sun up to sun down that was all he experienced. Sometimes she would send him on an errand and when he returned, complain that because he was gone the clothes had gotten wet, or she had to go outside and get the mail from the mailman. He was responsible for everything that happened, even when he was not around to prevent it. She was a brutal woman and I don't know how anyone could have loved her.

Andrew jr. and Ana were disrespectful to Adrianna, and they became quite adept at abusing old Andrew themselves. Complete with Adrianna's high pitch voice, the two of them added to his distress. "Grandpa, you didn't hear granny say to carry the bucket to the back? Grandpa yuh shoes dirty. Dohn bring that dirt inside." Why not? I wondered silently, he is the one who will clean it up anyway. "Grandpa, yuh really is a dam fool." One had to wonder why this man had tolerated this treatment from his wife for so many years, then from his daughter, and now from his grandchildren. No one ever heard him raise his voice even once in all of these circumstances, which took place daily and within earshot of all who could hear. If he was ever angry or embarrassed, no one ever knew.

Meanwhile, on the other side of the ocean, Ken finished school and pursued the career of his choice. He and Joan had two more children, one boy and a girl. When Joan finally returned to Trinidad, 25 years after her departure, it was because she had been ill, feared for her own survival, and decided to come to see her forgotten children (or more accurately, to let her forgotten children see her). The children were now adults and their relationship with her was awkward. After Ana met her, I asked her what she thought of her mother and she said, "I like her, she seems like a nice person." I don't know what I expected her to say or why her response stayed with me all these years. I am sure she would have liked her no matter what she appeared to be. These children had lived their entire lives holding on to a dream—a dream that a mother, who left them and who claimed to love them, would come and take them in her arms and they would be together forever. These children spoke of going to England long before they knew where England was. They were always planning and dreaming and telling everyone about their impending trip after their birthday, or before Christmas, or in the spring. Sometimes they had specific departure dates, but all ended the same way -in disappointment.

When Joan actually came for the visit, it had been years after I had been married, had children of my own, and was living again in Trinidad, quite a distance from my parents. On that particular day, I had been visiting my parents who still lived next door to the family. When my mother told me that Joan had come in the night before, I was very excited and impulsively rushed over to see her. When I got there, however, she was not in. I chatted with Ana who had by now spent several hours with her mother. I was anxious to talk to her about the meeting. I don't know what I expected to get from her, but I know I was hoping for something more from her than her simple statement about liking her. In the course of my conversation with Ana, I remembered and recounted to Ana (but mainly to myself) the experience of Joan leaving that night so many years before. I recalled how I had watched them grow up without their parents with the knowledge that they were alive and well in another country and had chosen not to come back for them. I relayed those feelings to Ana and later to my mother, and in the end I was glad that Joan had not been at home when I visited. I realized that I really did not have any desire to see her then, or ever again, and I never did.

Open Mango Season

As if Andrew Peeley was not being mistreated enough by his own family, my two younger brothers decided to have some fun at Mr. Peeley's expense. as well. They would take up positions far away from each other and one would call out loudly to Mr. Peeley. As he would move toward the sound of the voice, the other would call and he would go to that voice. They would repeat this, all the while laughing at his obvious confusion. Often one voice would come from the sidewalk outside Mr. Peeley's gate. Poor Mr. Peeley could not be sure that it was not a passerby. Despite any suspicions that he might have had about my brothers, without proof, he could not lodge a complaint to my parents.

One day, however, they got caught. My brothers, Allan and Mark, were identified as the mischief makers. This time they had not been merely calling and confusing Mr. Peeley, they had gone one step further. Mr. Peeley was washing some items by hand in a bucket, unaware that my brothers were spying on him over the wall that divided our two properties. Allan and Mark had a good vantage point to view this activity and they laughed and made comments as he washed the items one by one. They thought that he would be unable to keep his eye on the wash and catch them looking over the wall at the same time. Mr. Peeley seemed to tolerate the taunts while they, in turn, escalated the attacks.

The breaking point came as he was washing his wife's underwear and the boys shouted in unison, "Bloomers too?" and burst out laughing. This was too much for Mr. Peeley. He put the underwear back in the bucket and charged over to our house. It was the closest thing to an emotional outburst that anyone had ever seen from Mr. Peeley. He was almost incoherent when he began to explain to my father what my brothers had been doing to him. My father, who was somewhat of a chauvinist and at best a very traditional man, could hardly keep a straight face as he heard the details of the prank. He was able to maintain enough composure to apologize on behalf of the boys but did not call them to face the charge and their accuser. When Mr. Peeley left, my father's best friend, who had been present for the entire complaint, could hold his laughter no longer. By the time Mr. Peeley had reached his gate again, my father's friend released one of his famous gut-busting laughs, which caused my dad to chuckle. I know that Mr. Peeley could hear the laughter and, if he imagined it was related to his complaint, I know he must have regretted having made it in the first place.

Later that day, my father called my two brothers and spoke to them about respect for adults in general and his expectations of them in this regard. He told them that they were not to behave that way to Mr. Peeley again, but his rebuke lacked conviction, and I know he had only spoken to them after he had a good laugh himself. He did not have the highest respect for Mr. Peeley in the first place, but I know he liked the old man and perhaps felt sorry for him as well. As the boys grew, so did the mischief that they did to poor Mr. Peeley. In their teenage years, one of the ways in which they made his life miserable was their strong affinity to his mango tree.

The Peeley family had a large Julie mango tree. The Julie mango is a hybrid fruit with a peach-like flesh that is sweet and just slightly tangy. Mangoes in the tropics are the queen of fruits. In India, the homeland of mango, it has been considered the "Food of the Gods" and in Trinidad we certainly understood that. When Mr. Peeley's mangoes ripened between June and August and fruited heavily, we were in heaven. Despite his best efforts, Mr. Peeley knew he could not lay claim to the fruit on the branches that hung over our side of the wall, but what upset him even more was that my young agile brothers would get into the main branches of the tree and raid the tree from *his* yard. They would climb the wall, alight on the sturdier branches that connected what we considered "our side of the tree" to the trunk, and from there they would have their choice from a wide selection of the fruit hanging from almost any branch of the tree. The tree was wide but it was not very tall, so maneuvers in the tree presented little risk of injury. They would execute their operations early in the morning or very late at night so that Mr. Peeley had little chance of seeing them. In fact there was little chance of anyone seeing them.

We had a cousin, nicknamed Boose, who came with his younger brother to stay at our home. They had both been going to a high school in our neighborhood and when their parents had to relocate very far away for employment purposes, Boose and his brother moved in with us so that they could continue to attend their high school. Nine children were only slightly more trouble than seven. Boose and his brother were supposed to go home to their parents on weekends, but their social activities often precluded that; and so they became, in every way, a part of our household.

August was the end of the mango season and the mangoes were now scarce. Only a few remained on the tree and no new ones were expected. The competition between Mr. Peeley and the five boys that were now in our household (my youngest brother was too small to be involved) was fierce. Everyone watched the tree carefully every day to identify the targets. Poor Mr. Peeley was frail and used a ladder to get to the fruit. This limited his ability and he was no match for the boys. Boose was particularly adept at relieving the tree of its fruit. We believe he had some kind of alarm system which allowed him to get up before everyone else. He moved stealthily out of the house, went over the wall, and onto the tree. The only person who would hear him was my older brother, Elbert, whose room was on the east side of the house and whose window was a few feet from the large encroaching branches of the mango tree.

The last few mangoes were going fast and Mr. Peeley was getting so few that perhaps he began to doubt himself that he had indeed seen mangoes where he believed he had. Maybe he just wanted evidence to substantiate his claim, when he came to make it, but Mr. Peeley began drawing diagrams of what part of the tree the mangoes had hung before they disappeared. One Saturday morning, Mr. Peeley must have set his alarm too, because, he claims to have seen Boose in the act of taking one of his last mangoes off the tree. Both Mr. and Mrs. Peeley had complained to my mother. My mother had, as a dutiful and responsible parent, told the boys how wrong their actions were and had asked them not to take the mangoes off the tree without first getting permission from Mr. or Mrs. Peeley. As dutiful and responsible children, they listened to her. However, no one complied.

That Saturday morning, Mr. Peeley was eager to bring his case to my father. Unfortunately for him, my father had an early appointment with the manager of the bank. In those days the bank still opened on Saturdays until noon. When my father returned from the bank mid-morning, Mr. Peeley was out doing his Saturday errands, which were numerous. After lunch, some of my father's friends dropped by and he left with them on a "boys' lime." To "lime" is to *hang out*, which usually involved drinking, talking politics, more drinking, jokes, and more drinking. By the time my father returned that evening, and Mr. Peeley caught up with him to lodge his complaint, dad was quite inebriated. He appeared to listen and comprehend as Mr. Peeley showed him the diagram with the branch where the missing mango had hung. Mr. Peeley made a general complaint about the raids that the boys made on his tree, but his anger and his specific complaint was against Boose whom he had caught that morning removing the specific mango. Poor Mr. Peeley was almost shaking with fury and frustration as he related his tale. My father gave him the assurance that he would address the matter seriously with Boose.

As Mr. Peeley closed the gate, my father walked unsteadily into the dining room, sat at the table and summoned the culprit to come before him. When Boose was seated, dad told him of the complaint that Mr. Peeley had just lodged. Boose knew that he had been seen that morning and was prepared for this. He vehemently denied that he had taken the mango as alleged. Dad was in too happy a mood to be upset, but he made it clear to Boose that he believed that he had done as Mr. Peeley had claimed and he was suggesting at least that he not do that again. Boose continued to repeat his claim of innocence. Dad held his position that he believed the charge had merit. Determined to hold his ground and doing his best to convince my father of his innocence, Boose got up from his seat, went down on one knee, made a cross with his two index fingers, kissed the cross and said, "Uncle, I swear I did not take Mr. Peeley's mango." Dad looked at him, smiled, and without missing a beat, he fumbled out of his chair, held the back of it for support, steadied himself, went down on one knee too, made a cross with his two index fingers, kissed his cross too and with an exaggerated slur in his voice he said, "Boose, I swear I have not had a drink for the day." Spittle flew from Boose as the laugh exploded from his mouth. He helped my father back to his feet and that was the end of the mango issue. The issue ended, but that story has been a family favorite ever since.

Out of the Mouth of Babes

*I*don't know if Boose was careless when he was doing wrong or if he did quite a lot of wrong and so had to get caught a few times. Some weeks after Mr. Peeley caught him red-handed on the mango tree, there was another incident. This one involved a bottle of wine.

My mother had been entertaining and had served wine to her guest. She had opened a new bottle of wine and after pouring from it, left the bottle unattended on the kitchen counter. Later, when my mother went to put away the bottle, she noticed that there was considerably less wine in it than there was after she had poured the two glasses for herself and her friend. As usual, she called us all together and asked us individually if we had taken wine from the bottle. The culprit was the infamous *Notme* (the character that was blamed for everything that went wrong). Whenever my mother would ask us: "Who did I ask to put away those groceries from the counter?" or "Who did . . . ?" the answer from everyone was always: "Notme."

My mother was about to give up on finding the culprit when my young, two-year old cousin spoke up. He did not say much and he did not speak clearly. When anyone was doing wrong and looked around to be sure there were no witnesses, this toddler was always discounted. In this instance, that proved to be a big mistake. After everyone had testified to their innocence, my mother sarcastically said, "Well I suppose the wine drank itself since nobody here drank it." Little Boose (his nickname—he and my big cousin, Boose, had the same first name and so both of them got the same nickname) surprised us all. He especially surprised the guilty party when he said, "Aunty, I know who tate e wine." My mother, glad for any information, encouraged him. "You know who took the wine?" He went on, "Yes. Bih Boo tate e wine. Me tee him." This was as clear as his two-year-old tongue could master, but it was certainly coherent enough for all to understand. Big Boose, visibly shocked and confused, tried to intimidate the toddler by asking him directly, "You see *me* take the wine?" Little Boose, who had been nothing but loved and indulged in our household, replied with strength and confidence: "Bih Boo doe lie, me tee you tate e wine." At that, Big Boose, rattled and embarrassed, walked out of the room. We all dispersed giggling. My mom was too amused at the way in which the truth had been uncovered to say or do anything. She just picked up the toddler, kissed him, and thanked him for telling her the truth. After that, everyone paid attention to the presence of the youngest person in the house.

Little Boose's role as chief witness in the case gave him a new status in our family, but it did not detract from his position of favorite to everyone in the home. He was much younger than my youngest brother and we were all happy to have a toddler in the house again. We were all old enough to take care of him and we all enjoyed doing so.

He was the youngest child of my oldest cousin and the only boy in that family of five. He had four older sisters. His parents had desperately wanted a boy, and his arrival was greatly celebrated by everyone. His parents doted on him as did his siblings.

Just before his second birthday he began to be ill a great deal. No sooner had he gotten over one bout of illness, another came upon him. In some cases the diagnosis was unclear. This lively, lovable, chubby little boy was becoming withdrawn and losing weight. His parents were confused and concerned.

One day, a neighbor who was known for her insight and good advice, informed my cousin and his wife that what was affecting the child was what she termed, mother *mal yeux* (pronounced mal jo). Mal yeux is a patois term meaning "bad eye" or "evil eye" It is a curse, which when cast on someone may result in illness. The person causing the mal yeux did not necessarily know that they were causing it and left untreated could result in death.

In this case, the neighbor explained that because Little Boose's mother adored her son so much, she was causing the illness. According to the neighbor, mal yeux caused by a mother was the worst kind, and Little Boose had to be separated from his mother to recover. Fearing that she might kill the son for whom she had waited so long, Little Boose's mother sought my mother's advice.

My mother did not believe the explanation for the child's illness, and laughed it off as nonsense, but she saw that he was indeed losing weight and not looking well. She agreed to take him for a few weeks and care for him until he regained his strength. While he was in our care, his parents and siblings visited him very often and he enjoyed the love and care of two households. With no child to take care of at home, his mother took a job outside the home, and it was this, not his health, that caused him to stay with us for as long as he did. No one in either home seemed to object to the arrangement and so it remained for more than two years.

During his time with us, he was our mascot, our child, and our prized possession. We paraded him in front of our friends, displaying all of his abilities, his latest dance moves, his cheeky responses or the new songs he had learned and to which he provided his own lyrics. On the other hand we were his always-available playmates, his protectors, his indulgent parents, and the Santas that met all of his Christmas wishes. The arrangement was mutually beneficial to all and we treasured the time that he shared our home.

The Blessing

My deeply spiritual, Catholic mother knew about days of abstinence (during which the faithful were expected to refrain from eating meat) that no one else ever heard about. Christmas Eve was one of those days. I personally believe now, and even then, that it was not invented by my mother but by whoever had passed it down to her. Whatever its origin, I believe its main purpose was to protect the Christmas ham.

In my family of nine, a cooked ham—no matter how large— would not have lasted very long without fortification. Steeped as we were in our Catholic religion, despite the temptation fed by the aroma of that ham cooking on the fire, we always waited the many hours prescibed to have our first taste.

During my childhood years, ham was considered a Christmas food. Ham had to be imported to the island and the merchants did not have much of a market for it outside of the Christmas season. Ham was a tough, salty, almost leathery item that came from England encased in a jacket of tar and further enclosed in a mesh bag, all of which had to be removed prior to cooking. The ham had to be soaked in water overnight before the long process of boiling for several hours.

The ham was cooked outdoors in a large deep tin, commonly referred to as a pitch oil pan, a tin that originally contained cooking oil and, once empty, could be had from the grocer for cooking the ham. These tins were also used to store rice, flour, crackers and other items bought in bulk by large families.

Regular cooking fuel was not used to cook the ham. Instead, a wood fire was built in the cavity created by a few large stones, which were placed next to each other in a type of circle. The pitch oil tin was set atop the large stones with the fire directly below the center of the tin. The fire was then stoked and kept burning for as many hours as it took for the ham to become tender.

Ham was expensive, rare, and difficult to prepare. As such, it was a precious treat and a favorite of everyone in the family. That's why, I believe, my mother persuaded us that on Christmas Eve we were forbidden by the church to eat meat. We had our first serving of ham after we returned from midnight mass. It was paired with thick slices of still warm homemade bread and washed down with a cold glass of rich, red, sorrel that had been fermenting for several days. This early morning rite was the official start of the Christmas celebration for us. It was at this time that those still young enough to be visited by Santa, and not old enough for midnight mass, would be awakened to partake of the ham and see if their Christmas wishes had been met.

Apart from abstaining from meat on Christmas Eve, the other difficult Christmas season ritual that my mother put us through was "the blessing." A blessing by definition should be a wonderful thing and a far greater delight than waiting for a taste of the ham. Given a choice, many of us easily would have waited another day for the ham if it meant we could avoid "the blessing."

The blessing, like the abstinence on Christmas Eve, is something I have not found one other person to be familiar with all these years. It was something entirely my mother's, and something that is indelibly ingrained in the minds and hearts of all my siblings.

Every New Year's Day my mother would call us together and one at a time she would have us kneel in front of her lap, the way we said prayers when we were very young. She would sit upright on a chair, place her right hand on our head, and give us her New Year's blessing. This seemingly uplifting experience was anything but that. As we grew older, we hated the blessing more and more. Everyone got up at the end of their special event visibly upset, the older ones sobbing discretely, the younger ones bawling openly.

The blessing was a "talk" that may have been spontaneous or was prepared in advance by my mother...we do not know. It contained elements of past, present, and future events, expectations and aspirations. Mom would begin by reminding us that we were growing up, and depending on the age, say a little of the particular features of that age. She would talk about being more responsible now as we were getting older, as the New Year implied. She would outline the areas that each person had to work on in order to become a better person and remind us how much she, dad, and God loved us, and how proud she was of us. She highlighted the things about which each of us could be proud. I was very helpful around the house, and did my chores cheerfully without reminders. I was glad to help the younger ones and I set a good example for them. I was ladylike, something that always got extra points on mom's chart, and I was very well organized. On the other hand, I had to work on being more respectful and not always arguing when I did not agree with something I was told. Others were commended for keeping their surroundings clean, helping the younger ones with homework, and visiting the sick, which my sister Lyn did on a regular basis.

These compliments and observations should have made us very happy and positive about the New Year. The problem, however, was that it was very difficult to pay attention to phases one and two of the blessing when we knew that the next phase was just behind. Phase three was the tear jerker and what caused us to develop an immense dislike for the entire blessing.

In phase three of the blessing, Mom would point out to us that no one knew when God would call her home and she would outline in very clear and simple terms what she would want of us should she be called home to God in that year. We were to remain committed to our faith and our religion. We were to be respectful and diligent, as she had taught us to be, but most importantly we were to stay close to each other. The older ones were asked to promise to always look out for the younger ones and the younger ones were to be obedient and responsive to their older siblings. Mom would remind us that she never knew her mother, a fact that we always found exceedingly painful to think about, and we marveled at how she never seemed sad when she mentioned it. Of course, as I grew older, I understood that my mother was too young to have had much memory of her mother. In addition, her life with her step-mother (her mother's best friend) and her father had been happy and comfortable (the two had come to-gether through their mutual love for my mother and eventually married—at least that is how the story has been told). There was no real sadness on her part when she talked about her mother. During the blessing however, this was just added pain for us to bear.

Mom drew, or at least we saw, a picture of ourselves, mother-less and sad, relying on her spiritual presence to comfort us as she assured us that she would be looking down on us and that we would be all right as long as we stayed close to each other and to God. As she spoke, she stroked us so tenderly and so lovingly; it was as if her death was imminent. My mother lived a full life and died at 90 years of age.

Though my mother did not have much recollection of her mother at the age of four (the age she was when her mother died), I surmise it was this early loss that gave rise to her always preparing us for her demise. We already knew her much more than she had known her mother and so she feared that, should she pass, we would have a more difficult time adjusting and so we needed to be prepared. Perhaps too, though this has never come up, since her mother died at the age of 40 she may have had concerns that she was not destined for a long life. Whatever the reason, it must have been very important to my mother to do this blessing every year, for despite all of our tears, she never let up.

As we grew older, we tried to avoid the blessing by distracting mom on New Year's day around the time that the scheduled blessing would take place. One year, we were pleased that we had successfully evaded the yearly ordeal, only to be told by mom at dinner on January 2 that she had been hurt and disappointed by the fact that none of us had sought her blessing the day before. Later that night, my older brother herded us all into her bedroom and with as much sincerity as we could produce, we asked for that hated blessing. It went on as usual, only one day late. After that we never tried to avoid it.

I think over the years the tears became less and though, not a completely happy memory, those blessings impacted me positively. When I had my own children I continued the tradition. My blessings on my children, however, were happy and positive. I continued the tradition of phases one and two but permanently put to rest the preparation for death.

Dance and Sing

My mother always took her responsibility as a parent very seriously. She viewed this job as one that she did in collaboration with God himself. He was a very big part of every aspect of her life and He reigned supreme in her child-rearing practices. I really believe this, and so I must believe that God directed her, or at least was in agreement when she used the belt on us as she often did.

Today the notion of someone beating a child with a belt causes strong, sometimes misguided, emotional responses and allegations of abuse. I do not need a psychologist's definition of abuse to justify or condemn my mother's form of discipline because it was motivated by love and administered fairly most of the time.

My mother kept a two-inch wide old frayed strip of cheap leather that had once been a belt and was now without its buckle, hanging between the wooden, rail-like frame that ran across the top of the entrance to the kitchen. The belt was long enough to hang over on both sides of the frame just low enough to be within my mother's easy reach. The strap, as it was called, was used more often as a threat than for actual discipline. It was, however, used often enough on the legs and behinds of her brood of seven, but never without just cause and usually after multiple warnings had been issued.

Some years ago, at a conference where well-intentioned, committed, and knowledgeable therapists were condemning the use of corporal punishment for children, I was asked about my view on spanking. I was not arbitrarily picked for questioning. I had raised strong objections when the presenter, fully believing what she said, explained that even one stroke of corporal punishment can have dire consequences to a child and that the practice was damaging.

I explained that in my home the rules were known to all. Also known were the consequences of breaking the rules. These included, but were not limited to, corporal punishment. No one ever got a stroke above the waist, except if that person chose to take it in an open palm, as they did in Catholic school at the time. When we were punished, our parents were usually calm and it was always clear that we understood what we had done to warrant the use of the strap. I say our parents, but in reality, corporal punishment was administered exclusively by my mother.

The presenter at the conference asked if being beaten did not make me fear my parents. That question was almost funny to me. My mother was the only parent who ever beat us and she was the one that was more openly affectionate, and the one whose rules were broken daily. In reality, the punishment was so ineffective that most of the offenses and the punishment happened over and over again. My mother beat a lot, raised her voice a lot, loved a lot, cared a lot, and we took it all for granted and all in stride.

Our home was a safe and secure place where we were confident that we were loved—though I must say that our parents, and many parents in those days, did not go about saying to their children, "I love you"—as is now seemingly mandatory. We never, ever doubted that we were deeply loved. We knew we were a priority in our parents' lives and their love and commitment were shown in all that they did with, for, and to us. Even now, at many gatherings, my siblings and I laugh ourselves into stitches recounting some of our childhood escapades, including the experiences with the strap.

One tale that is always a crowd pleaser is the story I like to recall about the *singing*. I had broken something precious—one of the few trinkets that my mother still had that had belonged to her father. Her father had been deceased for many years and his memories were very special to her. Because her mother had passed away so early in her life, she had been especially close to her father and everything that reminded her of him. I felt badly about breaking the item, but I did not think that physical punishment was warranted. There were very few occasions where I think my mother had been unfair, and this was one of them.

After she had lamented the broken item, she informed me how I would be punished for my carelessness. Unfair as it might have been, I had no choice but to accept the decision. While I was waiting for the punishment to be implemented, I made a decision. I thought that I would take a stand against the injustice by not crying when I was hit. I figured that my mother wanted me to hurt and cry for breaking the memento. Well I would show her. I wouldn't shed a tear. Further, I made a bet with my older brother that not only would I not cry when the time came, but instead I would sing "Teddy Bear's Picnic," an old campfire song I knew.

Under the best of circumstances, with a voice coach, a piano and a full choir to accompany me, I cannot carry the simplest of tunes. Whatever gifts God had bestowed on me, a melodious voice was not one of them. I was feeling very smug with my decision and awaited my mother. When the time came, my mother held the strap, and explained to me in a way that must have made sense to her, why she had to punish me. As I held out my hand for the first stroke, I broke into song. To hear me trying to sing a happy song in a perky manner, my notes punctuated by the sound of the strap, and to watch my convulsive movements each time the strap stung my bare palms, was truly epic.

My brother, with whom I had made the bet, had taken a ring side seat for the event. He did not believe that I could really pull it off. After the first stroke of the strap and the first note, his eyes widened in surprise and amusement. My mother, unaware of the bet and my plan, was completely thrown by my bizarre reaction. Normally, I would have been hopping around trying to avoid the strap and crying loudly. I had this theory that if one cried really loudly it would move my mother to issue fewer strokes. Today, I was jumping around, that was as usual, but instead of crying, I was doing what passed for singing. My gestures were truly comical.

Unlike my brother who had been somewhat prepared and so was able to control his impulses, my mother was taken by surprise and responded with a burst of laughter. The punishment was prematurely ended and my mother remained all evening with laughter seeping out of every fiber of her being. With my siblings, I was somewhat of a hero. I belted the song and beat the belt, and I was pleased to turn my mother's loss into mirth.

Mark the Spot

More than 20 years after I had migrated to the U.S., my siblings and I were visiting our cousins in Canada when friends of theirs dropped in for a visit. After the introductions, we found out that one of them, Jennifer, had lived in Trinidad and was the sister of a neighbor in St. James. Jennifer was already an adult during her frequent visits to her sister, so we did not know her well and only vaguely remembered her these many years later. She, on the other hand, remembered most of us very well, but said the most memorable person to her and her family was my younger brother, Mark. She said that she recalled my mother calling Mark by name all the time and that she heard his name being called more often than all the other six of us combined. We laughed and soon everyone took turns recalling their favorite story about that mischievous sibling.

One of the stories that we all remember fondly is the one about the *spit in the sun*. In our home mom took care of the discipline or at least that is how it was presented to us at the time. We know now that in the more difficult cases of misbehavior, mom consulted a lot with dad and then presented the decision as her own. In fact, when she was challenged by us on some directive or decision that she was handing down to us, and she could not withstand the barrage of questions or objections she would say, "If you don't like it, go and ask your father." That, of course, would put an end to all objections and questions. As my older brother became an older teen, my mother sometimes enlisted his too-willing help in enforcing some of her rules. Although I've presented this as a general policy, I really only remember her asking for Elbert's help a couple of times in getting Mark to toe the line.

It had always been a difficult task for my mother to get Mark to clean the back yard. The yard was paved with concrete and so paper and fruit skins that may have blown or otherwise found their way into the yard, needed to be swept away often. My mother only asked that the yard be swept once per week—on a Saturday. The yard was less than 1000 sq. ft. in size and that included the covered area on the west side that was the garage and the enclosed area on the east side where the former owner of the house kept their horse. This left quite a small area that actually needed to be swept and kept clean.

While the area in question was paved, numerous cracks and holes of different sizes had developed over the years and were filled in with weeds. In the tropics, vegetation was lush and so weekly weeding of these isolated areas made the job more difficult than just sweeping, but most certainly it was not a full day's task. Accounting for the heat of the day and a slow pace, this task could be completed easily in just over an hour. Each Saturday morning, my mother began by setting my brothers to the task and when it was Mark's turn, she often ended the day threatening no dinner until the job was completed.

My two middle brothers, Allan and Mark also took turns emptying the garbage nightly in addition to cleaning the yard on Saturdays. When it was Allan's turn, it went reasonably well. Sure, he had to be reminded nightly to empty the garbage and on

Saturdays he would drift from the yard duty into conversation or play with neighbors who dropped by, but it was generally completed well before afternoon. It was also reasonably well done. However, when it was Mark's week to complete these chores, the frustrations escalated. Mom was constantly giving him reminders to take out the garbage beginning after dinner and continuing until bed time. My mother, in an attempt to instill discipline, would calmly wake Mark, as late as 10 p.m. before she turned in, and order him to take out the garbage. Dazed with sleep and rage, and staggering so that he could barely see in front of him, Mark would take out the garbage and hurry back to bed.

There came a time when instead of taking the garbage to the front of the house and getting back to bed, Mark decided to toss the bag under the house and return even more quickly to bed to continue his sleep. Before long, the vile odor of decay surrounded the premises. My mother alone at home one day, and unable to bear the stench any longer, set out to discover its source. She was very angry when she discovered how Mark had been disposing of the garbage, and it was clear that this had been happening over a long period of time. Mark had a huge mess on his hands. He had to remove the garbage item by disgusting, decaying item, since the bags that had once kept the rubbish contained, had disintegrated and were now part of the smelly heap. For this task of cleaning the garbage, Mark was not allowed the luxury of delay. As soon as he came in from school that day, he was set to it. My mother brought out a comfortable chair, placed it as far from the heap as she could but in full view of the project. It was a quiet evening, and my mother sat comfortably, with some sewing in hand, and saw every last piece of food, utensils, paper and vermin removed from beneath the house, re-bagged and properly disposed. While Mark—the sole engineer of the project—was busy, the siblings, who were so inclined, found excuses to pass by the site, make jokes, and poke fun at him. My mother pretended not to see or hear these exchanges, but her ample bosom would vibrate and we knew she was laughing.

On another occasion, mom enlisted Elbert's help in getting Mark to clean the yard. Elbert first tried to reason with him calmly to perform the task. That did not work any better than it did when my mother had tried earlier. To appear very stern, Elbert raised his voice. Mark seemed to take pleasure in not responding to that either. After some time had passed and there had been no discernible change in the condition of the yard, Elbert called Mark, took a piece of chalk and drew a circle on the ground. "I will spit here in this circle; and if this yard is not swept and clean, by the time that spittle dries, there will be trouble." With that Elbert went back to the porch with his friends. After what seemed a reasonable time, he went to the backyard to check on Mark, but the yard was still not clean, and Mark was playing in a corner with marbles. When Elbert walked to the circle, he noticed that the spittle had not yet dried. He was surprised, but realized he was not entitled to say anything since, according to his own conditions, the clock only stopped running for the job when the spittle dried.

Half an hour or more went by and the scene was the same. Mark was relaxing, the yard was not clean, and the spittle was still wet. This was a scorching hot day with ample wind. Moisture could not withstand those two elements for such an extended period. Elbert realized that something was amiss, so he found a spot from which he could observe Mark without being seen. Twice, at intervals of about five minutes, Mark would leave his marbles and observe the spittle then resume his game. The third time he went and stood observing the spot where the spittle was, but this time he looked around in all directions then stooped, bent his head over the circle and carefully spat in the same spot where my older brother had done the same.

From his observation point, Elbert shouted, "Aha! Caught you!" Mark was surprised and taken aback as Elbert charged toward him, angry at being played with by this child eight years his junior. Mark put his hand up in surrender, grabbed the broom, and hastily began sweeping the yard. He not only did a good job, he did it in record time.

The Ceiling Conversation

*I*t was Saturday morning. My parents were both in the kitchen talking about mundane domestic things and I was washing some fruit at the kitchen sink. I don't recall hearing footsteps on the roof. The first and only sound I heard was of the ceiling bursting open. Startled, I looked up to see two legs dangling from a large hole in the ceiling and pieces of debris falling to the floor. My mother's expression mirrored my feelings of shock and dismay, followed quickly by the sign of the cross. My father's back was to me, so I could not see his face, but he approached the hole and the two dangling legs, tilted his head upward, and began to talk to the owner of the legs, which by now I had identified as belonging to my younger brother, Mark.

I don't know what business Mark could have had on the roof of the house; how he managed to hoist himself up on to the gabled roof, which was quite high; or how he walked across the galvanized zinc panels, which would have been unbearably hot in the daytime sun. No answers were forthcoming and my attention drifted back to the voices in the kitchen. My father's tone and demeanor made the conversation seem so normal that anyone overhearing them would never have guessed that one of the participants was suspended between roof and ceiling with bloody legs hanging over the other speaker.

"Boy, what are you doing up there?"

"Nothing, Daddy."

"What do you mean nothing? What were you doing on the roof?"

"I was just walking, Daddy."

"You were walking on the *roof*? Is there a sidewalk there that I do not know about?"

"No, Daddy."

"I want to know what you were doing up there!"

Now, my mother, aware of how incongruous the situation was, stopped my father saying,

"Fred, let him come down from there."

My father calmly ended the exchange with, "Boy, get yourself down from there."

Once I realized that my brother was not hurt, except for a few layers of skin lost on one outer thigh, which was bleeding, I found the situation very comical. Watching my father talking to two dangling legs hanging just over his head and hearing my brother respond as if this were a normal situation really amused me. I am sure I saw a smile come alive on my mother's face as well, as we waited to hear Mark's story.

Back safely on the ground, Mark said he had just been curious to see what the neighborhood would look like from the roof, so he climbed onto it and explored the view from different vantage points. This was consistent with Mark's personality. He always enjoyed doing very daring things and seemed not to fear the consequences.

I recalled once when he put "hot ice" (sodium acetate) in a glass bottle just to see what would happen. Well, what happened was that the bottle exploded and he received severe cuts to his face and neck. While still recuperating from these injuries, he told me that now that he knew the glass bottle presented a danger, the next time he would put the "hot ice" in a plastic bottle. Many people would have chosen not to play with hot ice ever again. Not Mark! Danger was his friend and risk, his buddy.

On another occasion he decided to tease the neighbor's German shepherd dog, outrun the dog to our gate, run in, and close the gate before the dog could enter. He was successful quite a few times, as he allowed himself a good distance from the dog and a shorter one to the gate. On the last run, however, the timing was close in shutting the gate on the dog. He slipped, smashed into the gate, and for his effort, received a severe gash just over his eye. This required a trip to the emergency room and stitches. Mark's only response to this was that he had outrun the dog every time.

Given these exploits, no one was surprised at his reason for venturing on to the roof that Saturday morning. Mark explained that once he was on the roof he discovered that he had an excellent view of the mango tree next door and the perfect vantage point to decide on his strategy for his next raid on the neighbor's tree. As he contemplated his tactical moves, he did not see that a part of the roof was rusted and fragile until it was too late. When his legs broke through the roof and the ceiling, he fell into a sitting position which saved him from falling all the way into the kitchen and sustaining more serious injuries.

After his irregular conversation with Dad, someone borrowed a ladder from a neighbor and held it against the roof to allow Mark to descend safely. Watching him come to the edge of the roof and angle his body to begin the descent was tense for us all. I could see my mother's face, taut with anxiety, as he came down with as much bravado as he could muster in light of his bleeding legs on which he tried not to limp.

Meanwhile, my father had returned to his room and his bed. He later had someone come in to repair the ceiling and the roof, but he never said another word about the incident to my brother or to anyone.

Characters of Our Time

*I*n the 1960s and early 1970s we may not have had people who actually lived on the streets, but we had our characters who were on public display for most of the day. They provided great diversion and sometimes, downright humor for passersby. The better known ones were Dumpy and Rita and Mr. Arthur.

Dumpy was a Peeping Tom and somewhat of a pervert. He was very ill-suited to his occupation since he was barely five feet tall. He was slim, always nattily dressed, and maintained his appearance under all circumstances. He spoke very little, very softly, and smiled far too much to have been completely sane. His was the first case of spouse abuse I ever heard of where the male was the abused spouse. His wife had been described as an amazon of a woman, with a significant overbite and an overgrowth of facial hair. She was said to have had very large hands and a very high level of energy. She was an excellent cook and a generous neighbor. These details were pieced together from various people who, it was said, knew people who knew her. However, no one who spoke of her had known her personally or had ever actually seen her.

Dumpy was at one time, very obese and because of his small stature, presented a comical appearance. At that time, he was employed in a motor vehicle parts company where he packed and stocked merchandise. One night, when he was at work stacking products, a fire broke out in the building. In the commotion and panic of the employees running to safety, boxes and products fell along the path that Dumpy needed to walk to reach the exit. He was trapped. His only avenue to safety was a small window on the floor on which he was trapped. The window was behind him and accessible with a few short steps. Dumpy made it to the window easily enough, but his girth would not allow him to access this route. He pushed his head and his shoulders through the window; but, try as he might, he could not get his abdominal area through the narrow opening. He tried with such force that he wedged himself in the opening so that he could go neither forward nor backward. The fire department was very prompt and the small fire was soon under control. Dumpy had not been in any real danger, at least not from the fire; but, the picture of him, completely stuck in the window, arms outstretched, was on the front page of the morning paper that reported the fire. The terror captured on Dumpy's face in that picture was nothing compared to the horror he experienced when he saw himself in the paper and when he had to deal with the cruel jokes in the aftermath.

Dumpy did not return to his job and was not seen for more than six months after the incident. When he was next seen in public, no one recognized him. He had lost all of the excess weight and seemed, in every way, a different person. The difference, except for the weight loss, was not necessarily positive. He hung around bars in very crisp attire, made lewd remarks to young women, and sometimes attempted to touch them as they passed by. He never worked at any job again and during the day he would periodically leave the bar area for long periods of time. It is alleged that this is when he would peep into women's homes.

As a result of his escapades he once spent a week in the hospital. He had fallen from a pile of junk that he put together in order to climb up to peep into the bathroom of a middle-aged, single woman in the neighborhood. He had to take himself to the hospital by public transportation because, when he was discovered on the ground wailing in pain, it was clear how the accident had occurred and no one was willing to help him. He stayed out of the public eye again for months after that. In fact, it was rumored that he had left town. Despite his long absence, when he finally resurfaced, he was teased mercilessly by those who knew what had happened.

Rita was a drunk whose closest friends were two half-starved mongrels she called Bitch and Maco. Name notwithstanding, Bitch was male and a very active male at that, judging from its behavior towards female dogs. Maco was quiet and listless. Both dogs were ineffective in protecting their owner/companion, Rita. They almost never barked and seemed scared of people. In their defense, they were not effectively protected by Rita either. Schoolchildren stoned and provoked them daily. All three, Rita and the two dogs, were badly behaved, subject to the elements, and showed no signs of being cared for by anyone. These characters and lesser ones came and went with time, and added their own flavor to the community in ways that made them well remembered.

Mr. Arthur was, by far, the most remarkable and entertaining of all the characters we found in St. James. I suppose it is because we had such a profound sense of respect for our elders in those times that even our crazy, openly psychotic, raving maniacs were addressed with respect. The form of address to Mr. Arthur, however, was where the respect ended. Mr. Arthur was not really treated with respect; but then again, in an odd sort of way, he was not really disrespected either.

We were in a period when the great movies imported for viewing in our part of the world, those that did well at the box office and were nominated for high awards, often left a lasting impression on us because of their rich historical overtones. It was the period in which Charlton Heston was making his mark in Hollywood in epic dramas like *Ben Hur, The Ten Commandments,* and *El Cid.*

El Cid was a great popular hero, a brave knight of the chivalrous age of Spain. He was given the title of *El Cid* (Lord, Chief) by the Moors. The adventures of *El Cid*, both real and legendary, provided material for many dramatic productions for centuries.

In 1961, the movie, *El Cid,* was a highly romanticized version of the life of this Castilian knight. The role of *El Cid* was played by Charlton Heston. At least, that is what happened in Hollywood. In Trinidad, Mr. Arthur claimed the role and the honor that accompanied it. Like Charlton Heston, Mr. Arthur was tall, but there the comparison ended. There was no commanding presence, no great voice, and absolutely no grounding in reality.

Mr. Arthur got it into his head that he was the star of *El Cid*. It is not known if he even saw the movie. His lack of lucidity would have made it difficult to discern whether he had any facts as they related to the movie. He beat his chest literally and figuratively and explained to all, who would listen, that the producers of *El Cid* had come to Trinidad specifically to see him and had begged him to play the main role. He explained how well he had been treated in Hollywood and how pleased everyone involved was, with the wonderful job he had done. He asked everyone he knew if they had seen the movie and insisted in knowing what they thought of his performance in the leading role.

Some young men in the neighborhood, not only went along with Mr. Arthur's delusion, but, took it even further than he would have himself. They told Mr. Arthur that he had been nominated for an academy award for his performance in *El Cid*. Some weeks later, they told him that he had won the award for which he had been nominated. In this he surpassed even Charlton Heston himself who, though highly acclaimed for the role, did not win an Oscar for it.

Mr. Arthur was delighted by the news. The group informed him that since he was unable to fly to the U.S. to receive his Oscar, the academy was sending a special envoy to Trinidad to present him with his award. Mr. Arthur was beside himself with joy. He told everyone, young and old, of his great success and of his celebrity status. Even my father, who seldom participated in idle pranks, indulged Mr. Arthur. Maybe it was himself he indulged, but he actually discussed, or more correctly, encouraged Mr. Arthur to discuss the movie and the upcoming award. Except when he was with his friends and adult family members, my father did not openly partake in expressions of mirth or frivolity. For Mr. Arthur and *El Cid*, he made an exception.

On the day appointed for the award ceremony, Mr. Arthur was impeccably attired in a suit that the boys brought him with their absolute assurance that it had been sent by the academy. The suit was in fact borrowed, without permission, from an unsuspecting father of one of the award organizers. Mr. Arthur was a well-built man and fitted easily into the suit. The suit was a dark color, double breasted as was the fashion of the day, and exquisitely tailored. Mr. Arthur was also provided with a shiny new watch, again borrowed from someone's unsuspecting parent and cleaned for the occasion. Mr. Arthur was not an unpleasant looking man and overall was a reasonably attractive figure in his clothes and accessories. He posed repeatedly for pictures that were taken over and over again by cameras that had no film or may not even have been functional. The flash was all that was needed. Mr. Arthur was walked briskly to the reception hall which was around the corner from where he was dressed. Speed was important here to avoid the suit being recognized by a neighbor who might report the matter to the owner.

The hall where the award ceremony took place was a pool hall. There was no pool table there and no one played pool as we know it now. It was a place where people went to place bets for sporting activities, like English football (soccer), which took place daily across oceans in England. It was also where bets were placed for our local horse racing events. The English betting was a daily event, so the pool hall was open almost every day, and men—women were rarely seen in these establishments, and certainly ladies never even walked on the sidewalk in front of these places—would hang about there all day placing bets, drinking beers, and talking about the latest issues in local politics, as well as the British parliament and Britain in general. When one's nation is a colony, the lives and activities of the colonial masters sometimes play a greater role in one's life than one's own affairs.

The pool hall was closed for business on Sundays, as were all other business places except for one pharmacy in the capital and a smattering of small businesses in rural areas—and they were not ever fully open to the public, but would transact some business to well-known customers through a back door, window, or hole in the gate. The pool hall was reserved for the award ceremony for Mr. Arthur because the manager was young and keen to be part of the fun. The weekly patrons of the pool hall had all been invited to the ceremony, which was scheduled for 4:00 p.m. on Sunday afternoon.

Following the award ceremony, my older brother, the only family member eligible to attend the event, gave us a detailed account of what had taken place. All I remember now, these many years later, is that there was a crowded room of young adults and teens; a few meaningless speeches by anyone daring enough to go forward; and the pool hall manager. He had donned a jacket and tie, for the event, and presented Mr. Arthur with a cheap glass vase. The vase was short with a wide scalloped opening, very heavy, and had a greenish tint. I know this because Mr. Arthur walked around with it for several days showing it not only to those who asked, but for a period he went door to door to be sure that the community was aware of his great achievement.

Mr. Arthur was never dirty, but on the days he was exhibiting his award, he seemed to dress with more care than usual. I can only say that I was more aware of his shoes, which though old and worn, were cleaner than usual. His hair glistened like drops of dew, the way oil or grease reflects light on wooly hair. He also wore a long-sleeved white shirt, like a professional or public servant would have. Climate notwithstanding, we followed the dress codes of our colonial masters. In due course, Mr. Arthur ceased to parade with his trophy and the brouhaha over *El Cid* subsided.

In 1966, Queen Elizabeth II was scheduled to visit our little island. It was not unusual for the British monarchs to make periodic calls to their protectorates, or in this case former protectorates. At least twice in the 20 year period of which I was conscious, we had visits from the royal family of Great Britain, as it was then known. In 1962, Princess Margaret, the younger sister of the queen, visited us on the occasion of our independence, and then in 1966 the queen came herself.

According to the information that the government issued for the 1966 visit, and which was repeated in schools across the country, this was a formal state visit. According to Mr. Arthur, this visit was a personal one. The queen, whom he claimed to have met and who was a friend of his, was coming for the expressed purpose of "looking him up" as she had promised. It was the first visit of the monarch, not as the sovereign leader of the nation, but merely as a visiting head of state.

Like most islands in the West Indies, Trinidad & Tobago became first a British sugar colony. Britain later capitalized on the island's lucrative cacao (cocoa) industry, which dominated the economy then. After the collapse of the cacao crop, the oil industry emerged and with it, significant changes. Soon Trinidad & Tobago was one of the many countries seeking to be released from domination by external powers and became an independent nation in August of 1962. The nation was under no obligation to our royal visitor, but being warm and friendly people, Trinidadians put their best foot forward. Preparations for the event went on for several weeks. The nation was energized and diligently focused on the event, so Mr. Arthur's claims of his special friendship and his preparation for the visit were unremarkable. I only recall that during the period leading up to the event, when my father would see Mr. Arthur, he would ask, "Mr. Arthur, how are the preparations going?" and Mr. Arthur would reply, "Good, good. Everything going good." The queen came and left and Mr. Arthur remained expectant of her visit to him. After a while, he stopped talking about it. I don't know what became of Mr. Arthur, but by the time I migrated to the U.S. in 1970 his place had long been usurped by somewhat less remarkable crazies.

Then and Later

S ome years ago, at the 25th wedding anniversary of my older brother, Elbert, a dear family friend recounted his relationship with my family. He said, "...from the beginning, I fell in love with the entire family. At the Guerin home one learned what family was about." He explained that our family radiated heart-felt warmth that touched everyone who called on them. He told the group that, "a visit to the Guerin home was like going to the movies or going to the race track with your pocket full of money. At the Guerin's, there was always a lot of laughter, a lot of music and jokes, jokes, and more jokes. There were always a lot of people dropping in just to bask in the sheer ambiance of that home...," he opined. He said that he considered the Guerin family the prototype for family life, and that in the Guerin home one learned how to nurture the bonds and promote harmony in a family from two masters—my parents. He believed that everyone who visited and spent time with us was profoundly influenced by the experience. He commended my mother for the aura of caring and warmth she exuded, and for being what he called, "The Essence of Motherhood."

All of this was probably very true from the point of view of visitors; for us, it was home and our family—nothing special. I think it is natural for a child to believe that everyone is like him or her, and that everyone's family is like his or hers. Since a large family was my only frame of reference, I believed that all large families were close-knit like mine and enjoyed spending time together. I did not know that getting together on Sunday evening, and dancing with each other to all the top ten tunes of the hit parade, was unusual. I thought that all big brothers were funny and protective. I did not know that when my big brother, Elbert, tried his best to make us laugh when we were upset, or regaled us on Sundays with every detail of the movie he had seen the evening before, his actions were not the norm. I also did not know that other big brothers did not ask their mothers to spank them instead of their youngest siblings, when those siblings misbehaved. I took it for granted that older brothers came to the hairdressing salon, if it was getting dark and a younger sister had not returned home from having her hair done. Every evening at dinner, as our family sat around the table and gently competed for the funniest events of the day—while my father sat at the head of the table trying to stifle his laughter—I thought that was the scene at dinner tables all over the island.

One of my aunts used to say that we could sell tickets to watch our family, and that we were better than television. I assumed that this was because she had no children of her own and so did not know what it was like to live in a large family.

We did seem to have a constant flow of friends coming and going from our house; but I attributed that to the fact that my siblings were quite friendly and popular among their peers and the fact that we were generally not allowed to go to other people's homes. This meant that anyone who wanted to hang out with us had to do so at our home. My parents never seemed to mind the steady stream of people at our home. As a parent myself now,

I realize that it was a small price to pay to know that your children were always safe. It also gave them an opportunity to assess our friends without ever seeming to do so. Just having the friends around so much and listening to our conversations, as well as casually asking questions of the friends in a very cordial manner, gave them information that was useful to have about the people with whom their children associated.

Interesting too are the countless examples of people who came to our home as a friend of one person, only to get so close to another family member so that after a while it was difficult to remember which member of the family was the original friend. In some cases, the secondary friendships grew closer than the first and alliances changed. That was never a problem for us, however. We were not territorial with our friends and liked the fact that they were comfortable with everyone in our home. We hung out with each other so much, anyway, that it was good when friends were able to work their way into the sibling dynamics.

Once, when I was a teenager, a friend of mine dropped by one Sunday afternoon and found the dance party going on. We were dancing to the Top 10 Hit Parade. It was a party with only my siblings—brothers and sisters or sisters and sisters dancing away. She commented on it all afternoon, as if he had never seen anything like that before. She did seem to consider it odd, and let me know that, but I was not offended. What did offend me was some months later, that particular friend planned a surprise birthday party for me; she invited my best friends and some of hers, but did not include any of my siblings.

Another time, in my early teens, I was invited to visit a large family who lived in the town of Arima. The family and mine were very close. There were a number of children in that family of six who were close in age to several of my siblings and me. I was very much looking forward to spending this weekend with the family. Instead of finding a home away from home, I found six individuals who seemed angry with each other all the time and who did their best to stay out of each other's way to minimize hostilities.

At mealtime they exchanged grunts across the table. The father's job took him away a lot and he was absent on that weekend. The mother was merely the seventh individual at the table. There was no conversation or comment, except to have a dish passed. No one seemed to laugh or even smile, and one had the distinct impression that all the members were anxious to finish their meal so that they could go back to their little corners, away from each other.

As a guest, I got no special attention or courtesy. The girl who was my exact age, and who I expected to have been my companion for the weekend, stuck her head in a book most of the weekend except for when she played the piano. She barely seemed aware of my presence. Her older sisters were patronizingly tolerant of me and I found myself drifting about the large compound hoping to find some way to entertain myself. No one seemed troubled by my discomfort. The house was just large enough for the family, yet it felt very vast and the occupants almost invisible. Each hogged his or her respective space in the house and boundaries were strictly respected. I was very surprised at what I found as this family always seemed to be a reasonable amount of fun when they visited us. I had such a feeling of isolation and loneliness and I counted down the hours to Sunday afternoon when I would go home to my family. It was the longest weekend of my life. I understood what it was like to be truly bored.

In general, children did not know the word *bored*, except as it referred to something being penetrated. Children were always active and always finding ways to entertain themselves. True, some of the activities were less than wholesome, like when we would climb a ladder to the roof of a 10-foot high shed in which we housed lumber, boxes, and in one period of our lives, ducks. From this shed we would, on a dare, jump to the solid concrete ground below. None of us were aware of the extent of the danger we were courting and no adult ever caught us at these daredevil games. None of us ever got hurt, either.

There was also the game we played the year one of the boys got a BB gun. We would take turns running in a zigzag pattern while others took turns trying to shoot us. One of our friends was shot in her upper thigh. We managed to keep this from the adults—her parents and ours—but, we did put an end to that game.

One of our favorite games, and a safe one, was called *Rounders*. When we played it, the five older siblings and some neighbors were involved. The game was, I suppose, a precursor to baseball in the Island, or more correctly, a Caribbean version of it, because baseball was already well established in America by that time and has never become popular in the Caribbean.

Our game did not require the use of a bat, though what we did to the ball (with clenched fists or open palms—depending on style) we called *batting*. The action was in fact closer to a tennis serve. The person batting began with the ball; it was not thrown to him. With hands held above his head, he batted it as far into the field as possible. The rest of the game progressed like baseball. Our yard at the time was very big, so getting to all the bases took a while. A game of Rounders could go on all afternoon. In addition to the extensive yard, which took time to traverse, each player on both teams had to have a turn at batting and running the bases. Boredom was not an option with family, friends, and wide-open spaces to play.

Something remarkable happened, after 1970, when I moved to America. In the early 1980s when we returned to our home, the yard had shrunk considerably. We could no longer even envisage a game of Rounders taking place there. The bases would have been very close to each other and the players would have had no room to build any speed running between them. It seemed that all they would have had had to do, was lean from one base and touch the other. How that shrinkage occurred, we do not know, but we all agreed that it had happened and that it had affected the entire property.

The large bedrooms seemed barely to have much room left after accommodating the furniture. The room in which we ate was so small that one would have had to be right up against the wall on one side to allow sufficient room for the persons on the other side to get in and out of their seats. Only the person at the end of the row would have been able to come in and go out comfortably with the other persons still in their seats. But no one remembered that being a problem years before when we were around that table every morning or every night. Our parents, who had remained in the house for the duration, saw no change in the size of either the house or the yard. They could not understand our confusion at all. Clearly it was just a matter of perception. As small children everything seemed huge and these large images were imprinted in our minds. As adults, we saw things as they really were.

In the 1980s, the house was not small but it was not as grand as it had seemed two decades before. Not only had the house and yard shrunk, but the houses nearby were ever so close together. If there were new "characters" in the neighborhood, we did not know them. So much had changed. So much of my old life no longer existed. However, what would never change; what I would not lose; what would not shrink or ever become ordinary, are those cherished memories of my youth—memories in which we loved, cared, shared...and then we laughed.

About the Author

The author L. Guerin-Cameron was born in Trinidad where she spent her formative years. She has since lived in the US, Canada and Europe and has travelled extensively. In spite of this however, she has always maintained very strong ties with, and affiliation to her country of origin. She returns there often from her home in Florida. Having formally retired from teaching she continues as a volunteer, to teach reading skills to adults.